PUBLISHED BY KOYAMA PRESS
KOYAMAPRESS.COM
FIRST EDITION: SEPTEMBER 2014
ISBN: 978-1-927668-11-5
PRINTED IN CHINA

KOYAMA PRESS GRATEFULLY ACKNOWLEDGES THE CANADA COUNCIL FOR THE ARTS FOR THEIR SUPPORT OF
OUR PUBLISHING PROGRAM.

CAT DAD, KING OF THE GOBLINS

BRITT WILSON

koyama press

LUEY, AGE 10

- LIKES BACON, READING AND HEDGEHOGS.
- PUTS UP WITH HER LITTLE SISTER HANGING AROUND REMARKABLY WELL.
- HER BEST FRIEND IS A FROG, HER MOTHER IS... NOT NORMAL, AND RIGHT NOW, HER DAD IS A CAT.
- WANTS TO BE INDIANA JONES WHEN SHE GROWS UP.

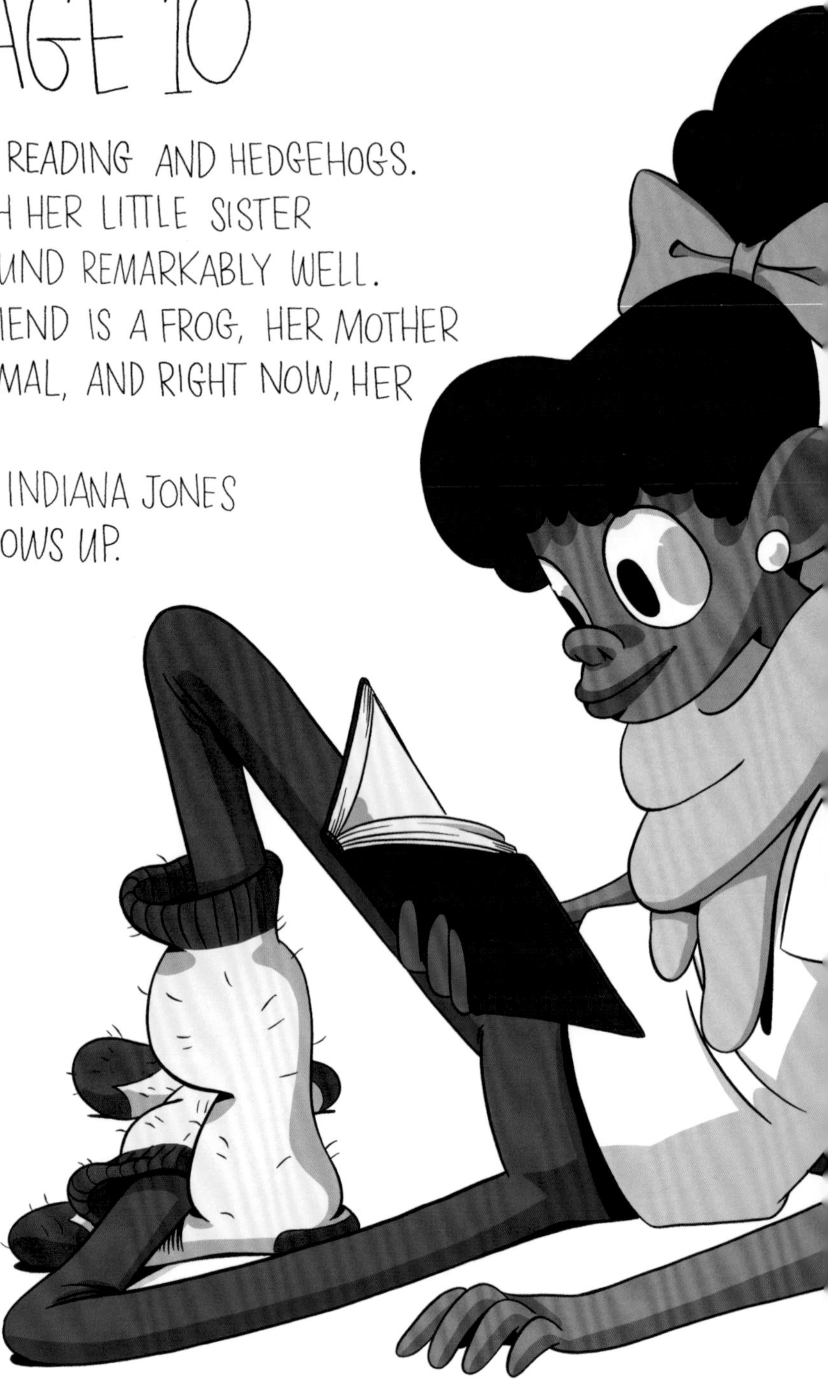

MIRI, AGE 5

- LOVES TO COLOUR.
- ALSO LIKES PLASTICINE AND SHRINKY DINKS.
- HATES BEING LEFT BEHIND BECAUSE SHE'S TOO LITTLE, SO SHE'S ALWAYS THE FIRST TO JUMP ON AN ADVENTURE!
- SEEMINGLY UNPHASED BY THE ODDNESS THAT RUNS IN HER FAMILY.

PHIL, AGE 10

- LIKES HANGING OUT AT LUEY'S HOUSE BECAUSE, DESPITE IT BEING A BIT ODD, IT'S QUIET COMPARED TO HIS HOUSE.
- HAS 500 BROTHERS AND SISTERS.
- DOESN'T EXACTLY HAVE GRACE UNDER PRESSURE, BUT HE TRIES HIS BEST.
- DOESN'T LIKE WEARING PANTS.
- WANTS TO BE A FOREIGN DIGNITARY WHEN HE GROWS UP.

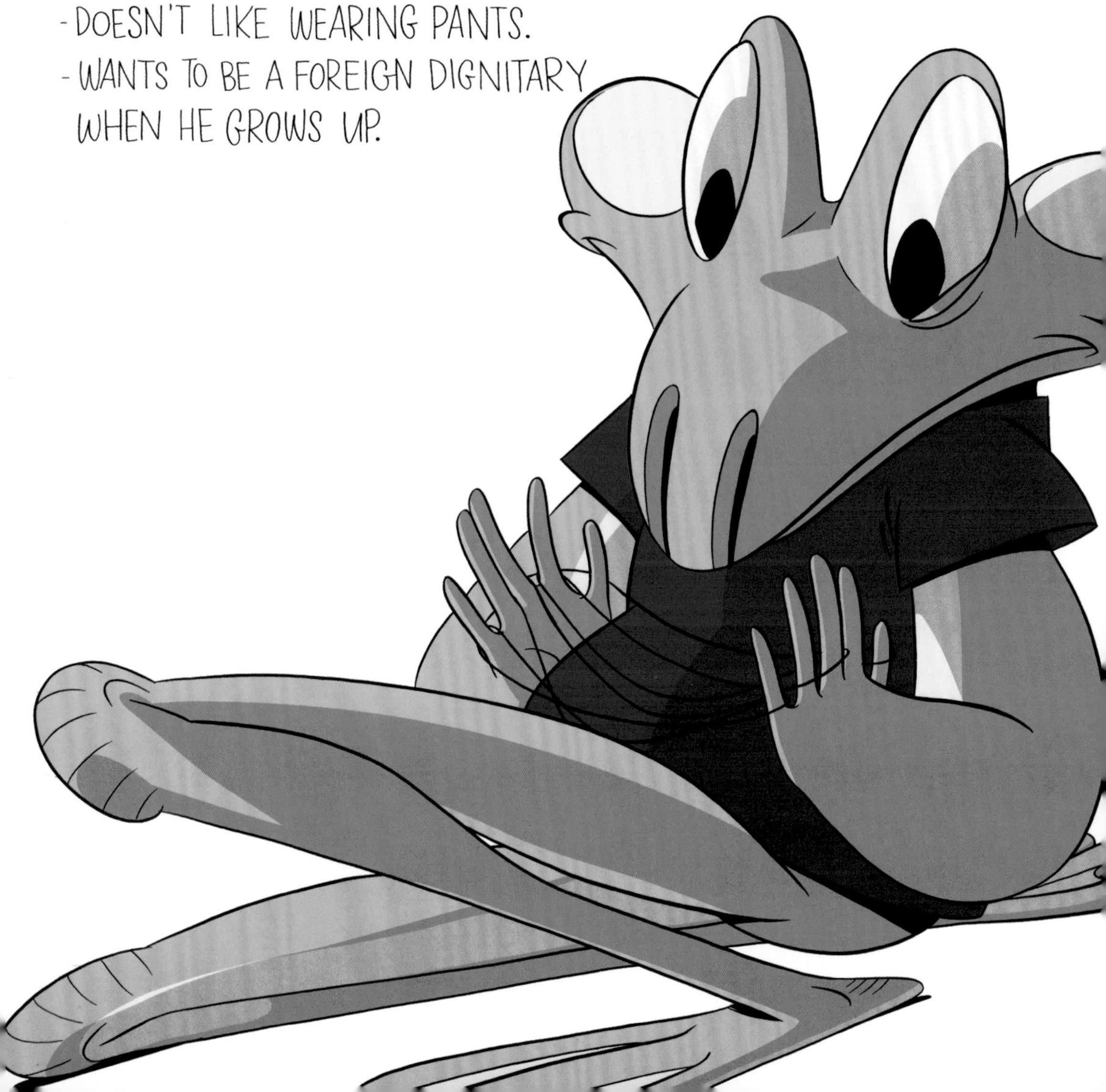

MOM

- SHE'S ALREADY A GROWN-UP, BUT HER JOB IS A MYSTERY.
- LOVES YOGA, AND EXERCISE CLOTHING.
- HAS AN UNNERVING TENDENCY TO DO THINGS OTHER MOMS DON'T (OR CAN'T) DO. LIKE TURNING HER HUSBAND INTO A CAT.
- ALSO HAS A TENDENCY TO "OVERDO" IT.

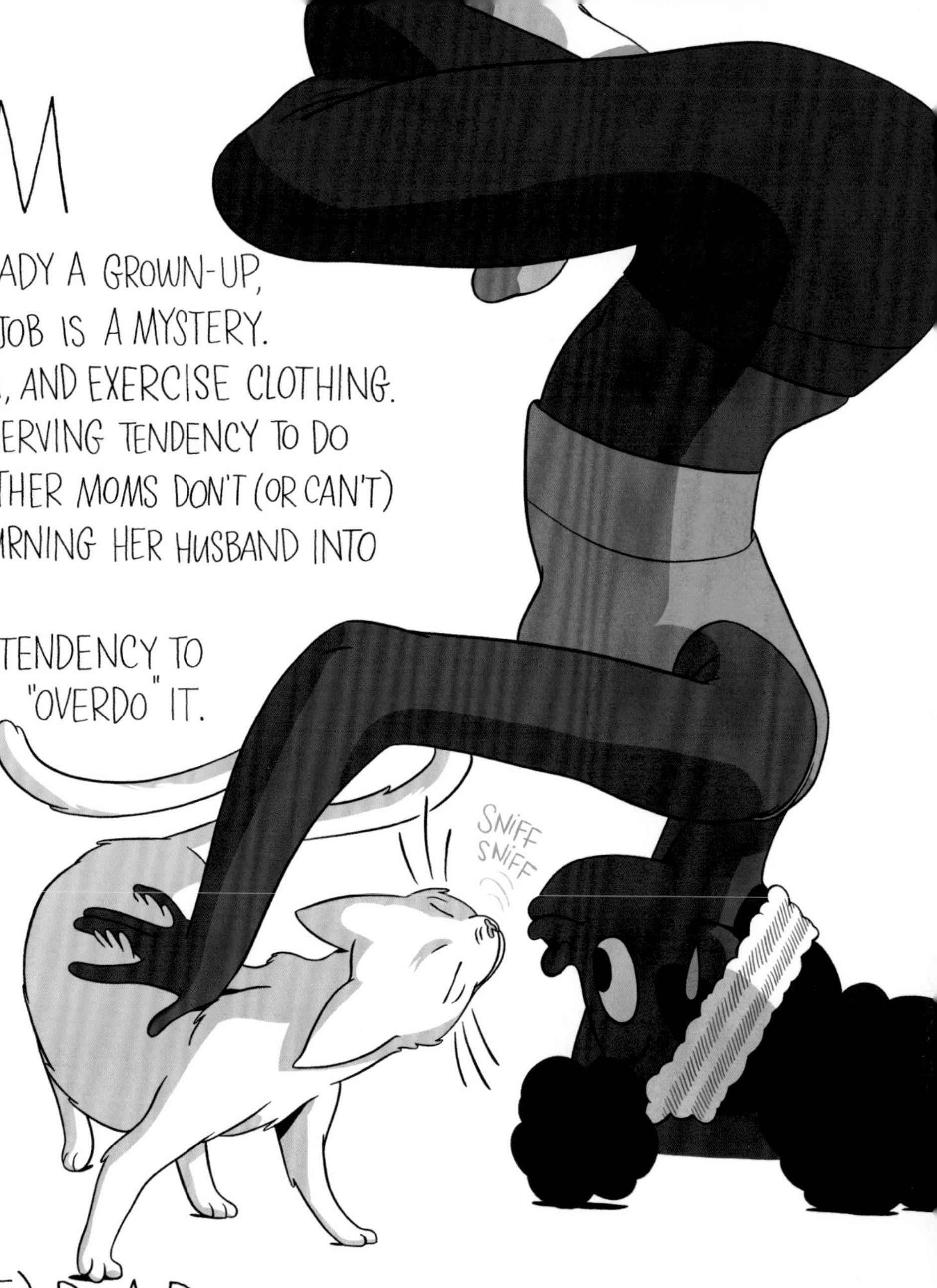
SNIFF SNIFF

(CAT) DAD

- RIGHT NOW HE'S A CAT. NORMALLY HE ISN'T.
- CURRENTLY HE HATES HAVING HIS TAIL PULLED, BEING RUBBED THE WRONG WAY, AND ANY AMOUNT OF WATER.
- HE LIKES: CATNIP, SLEEPING IN WARM LAUNDRY, STRING/YARN/RIBBON/TWINE

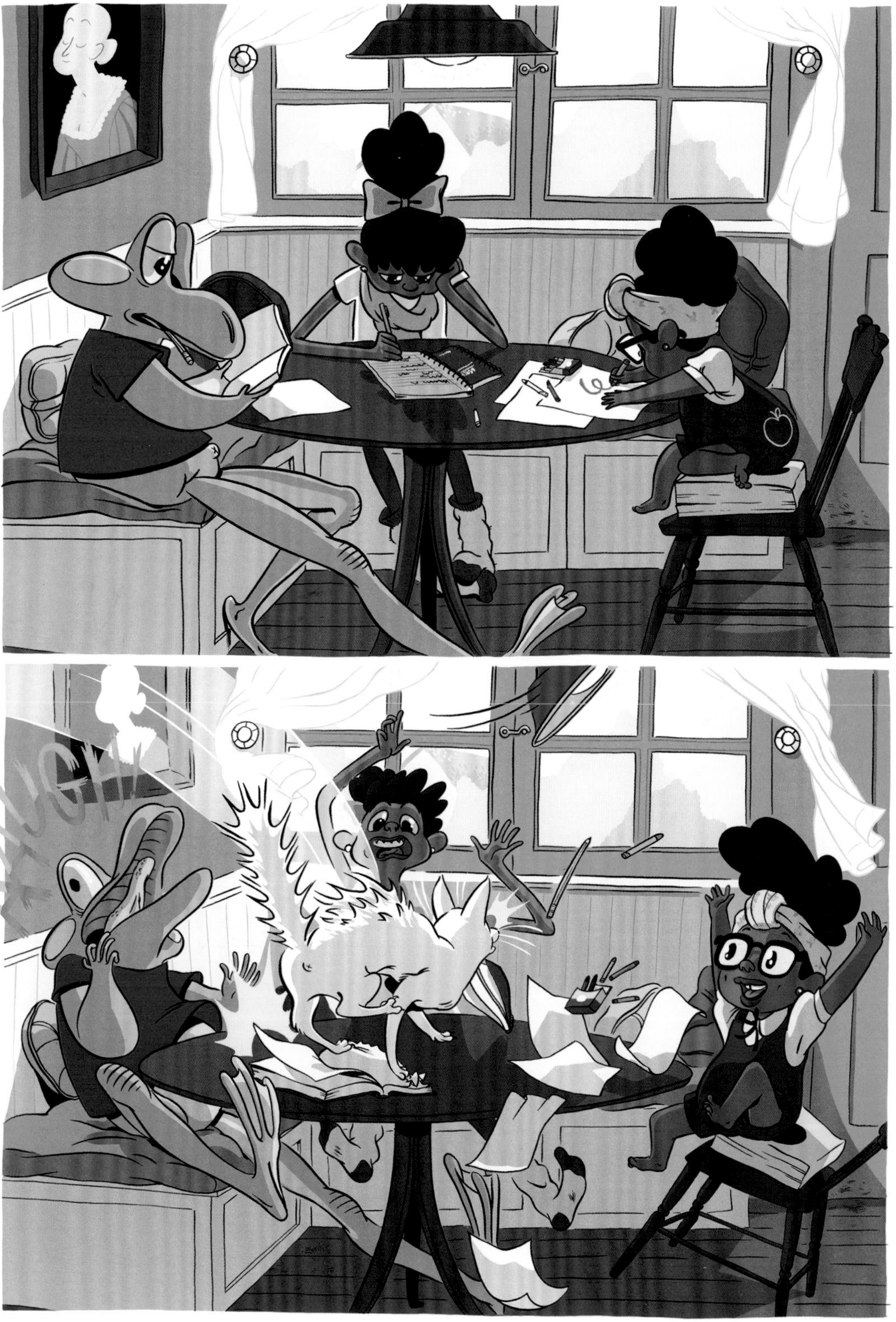
AAUGH!!

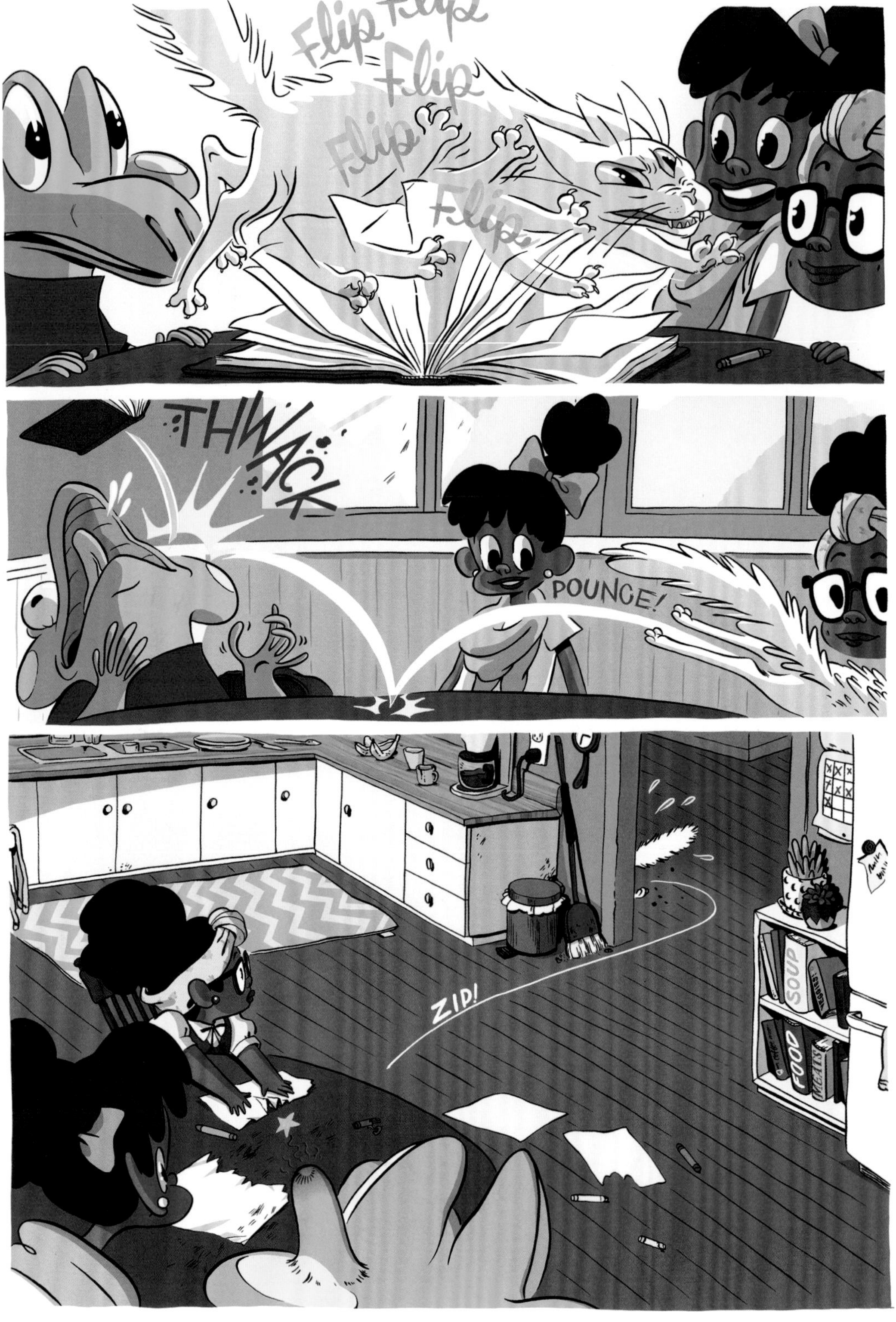
Flip Flip
Flip
Flip
Flip
THWACK
POUNCE!
ZID!
SOUP
FOOD

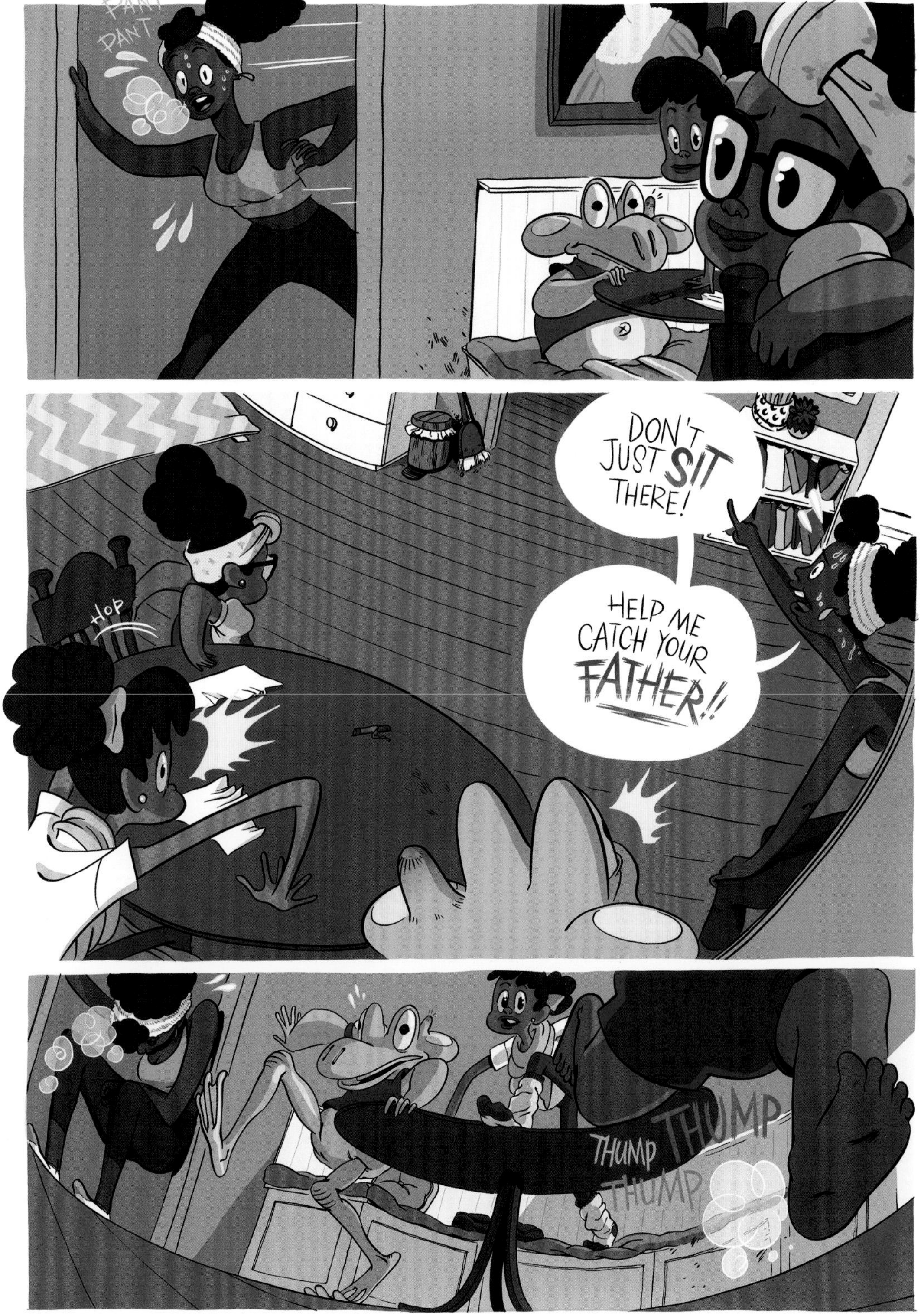
PANT PANT
DON'T JUST SIT THERE!
HELP ME CATCH YOUR FATHER!!
HOP
THUMP THUMP THUMP

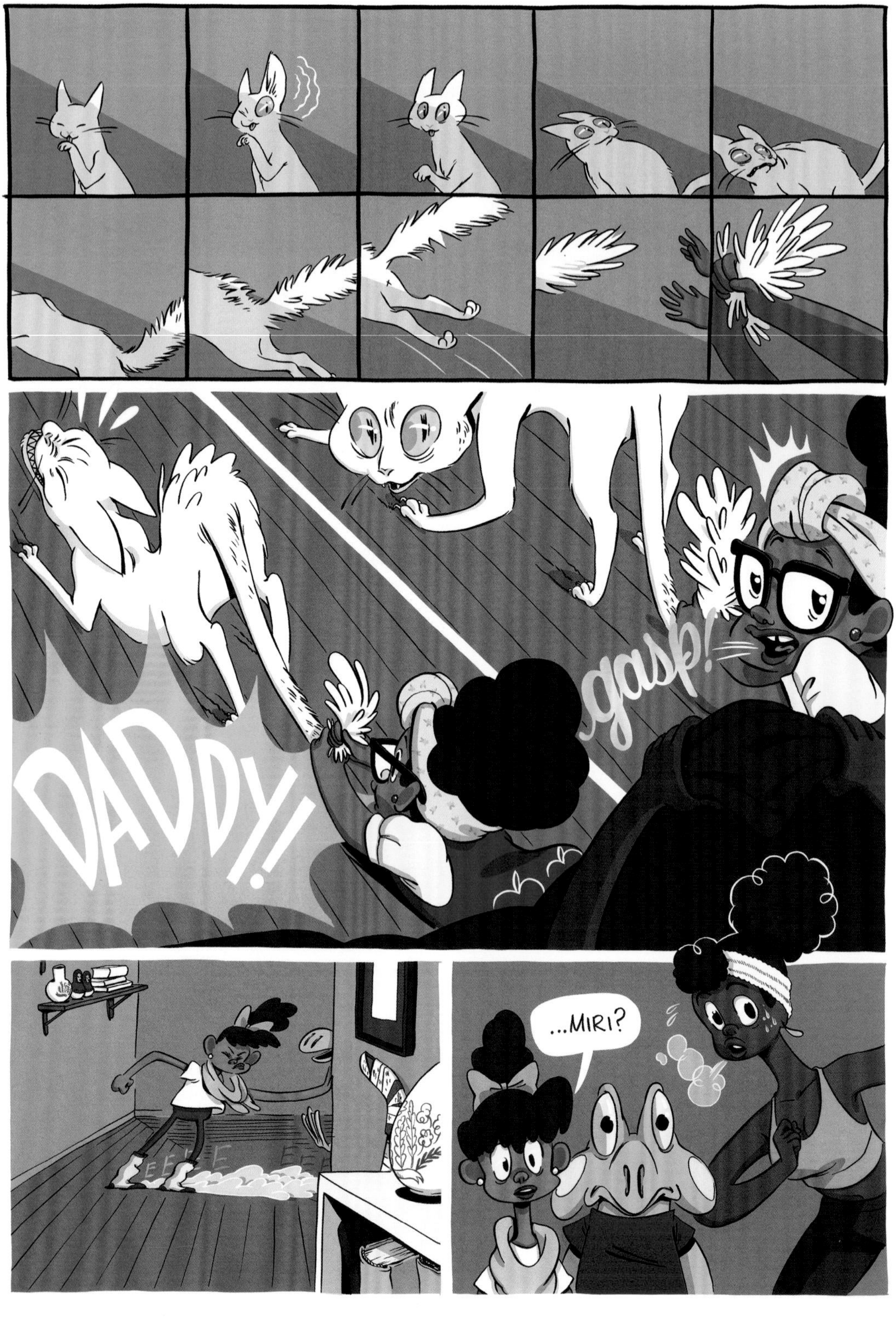
DADDY!!
gasp!
...MIRI?

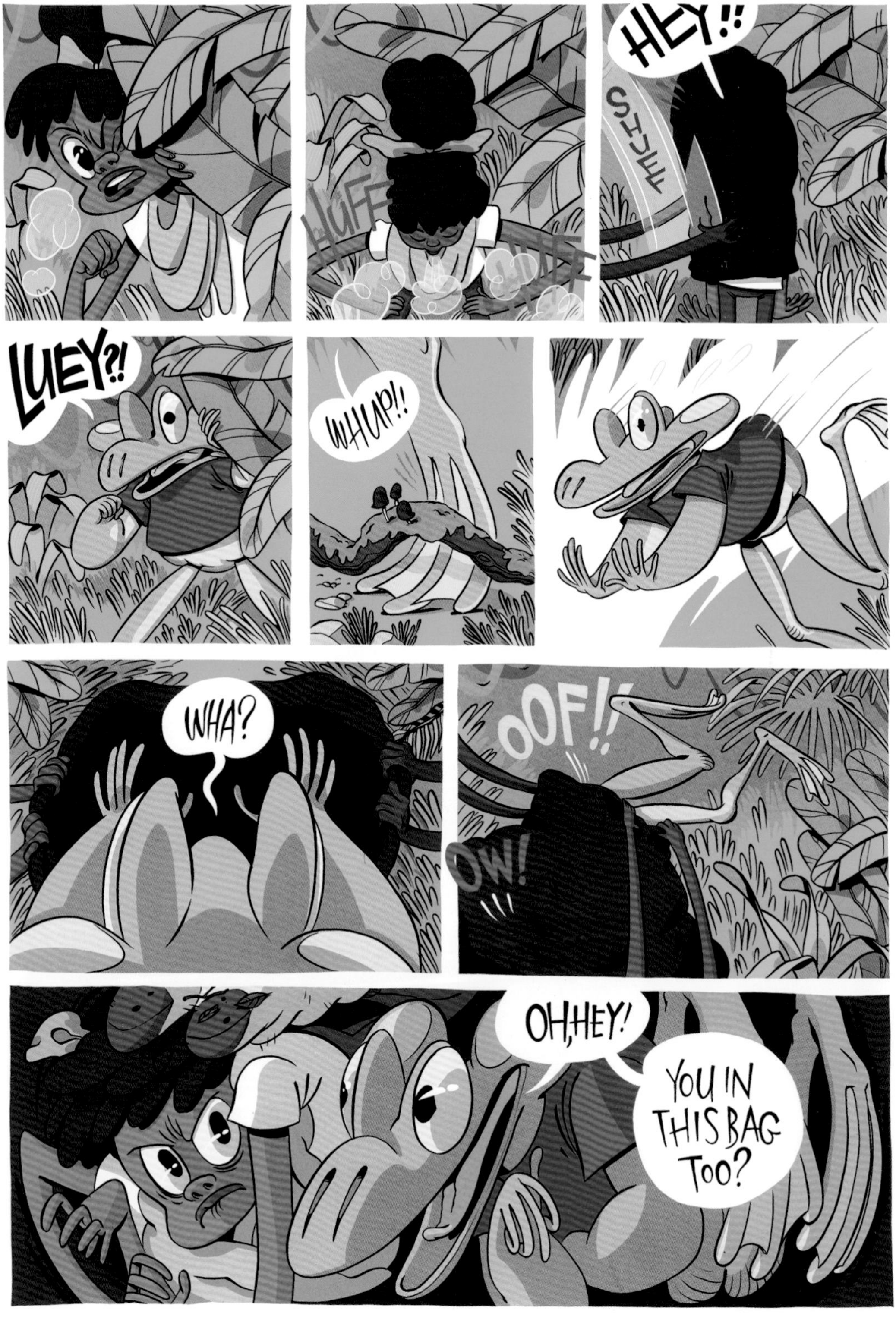
HUFF
HUFF
SHUFF
HEY!!
LUEY?!
WHUP!!
WHA?
OOF!!
OW!
OH, HEY!
YOU IN THIS BAG TOO?

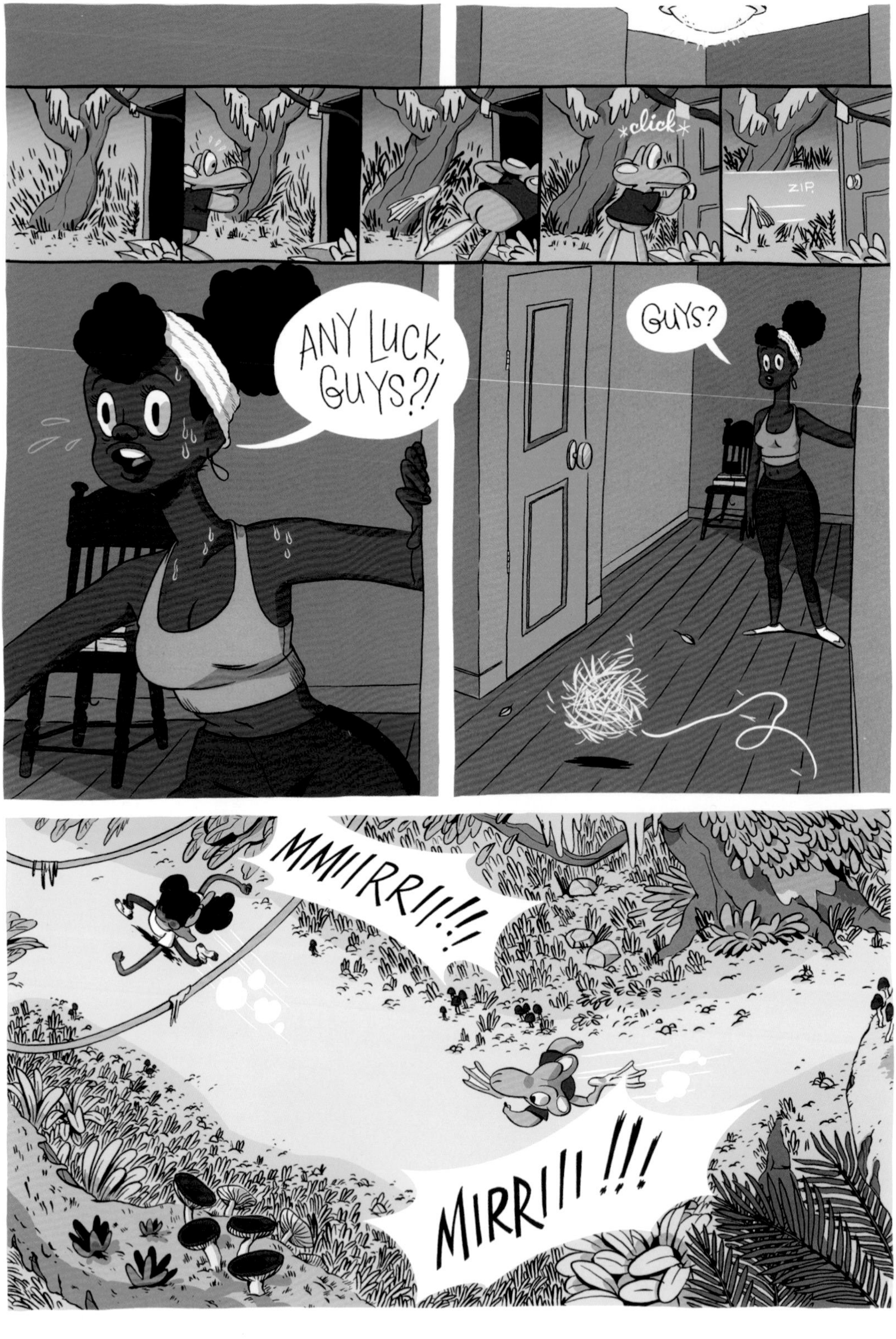
click
ZIP.
ANY LUCK, GUYS?!
GUYS?
MMIIRRII!!!
MIRRIII!!!

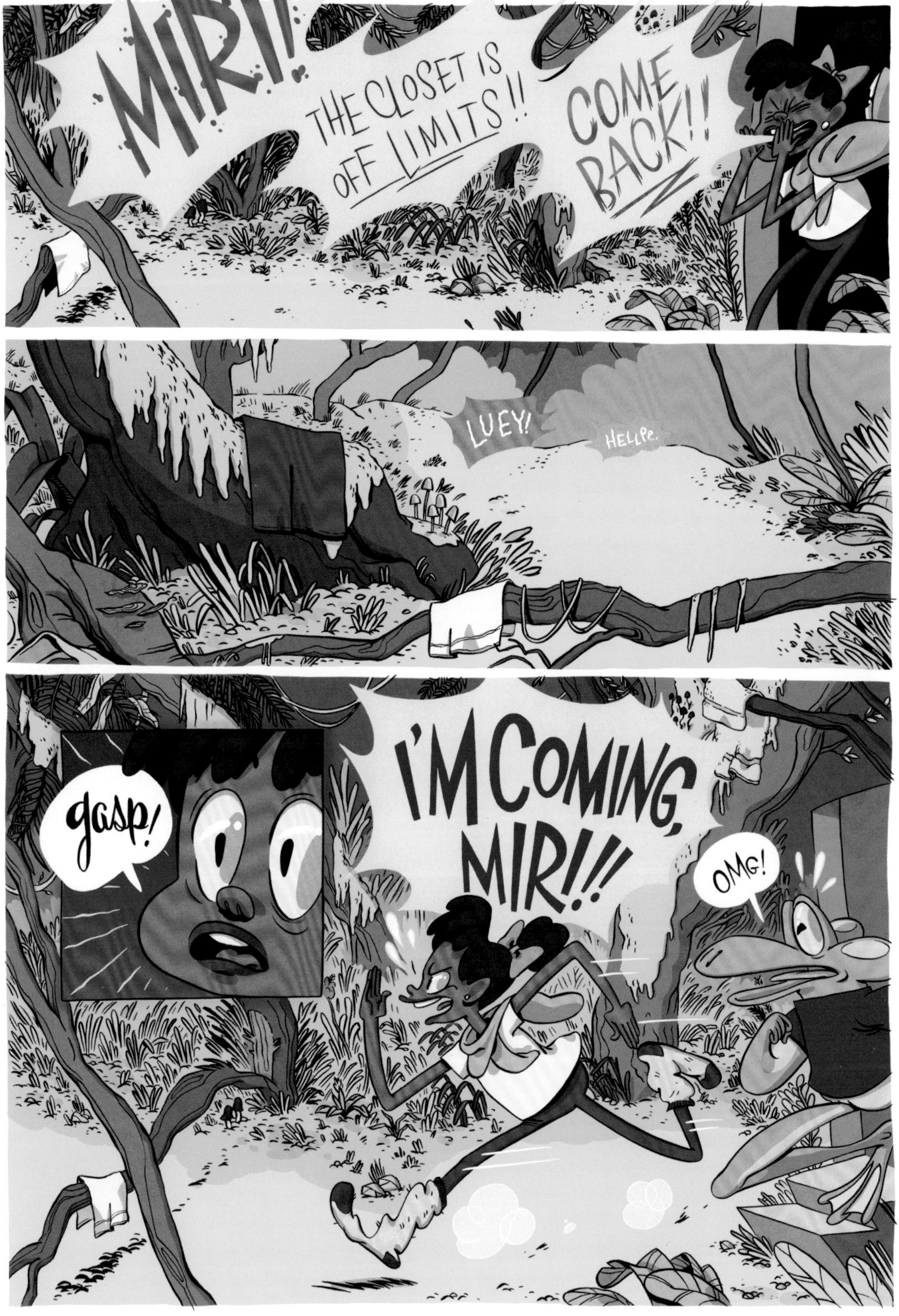
MIRI!
THE CLOSET IS OFF LIMITS!!
COME BACK!!
LUEY!
HELLP..
gasp!
I'M COMING, MIR!!!
OMG!

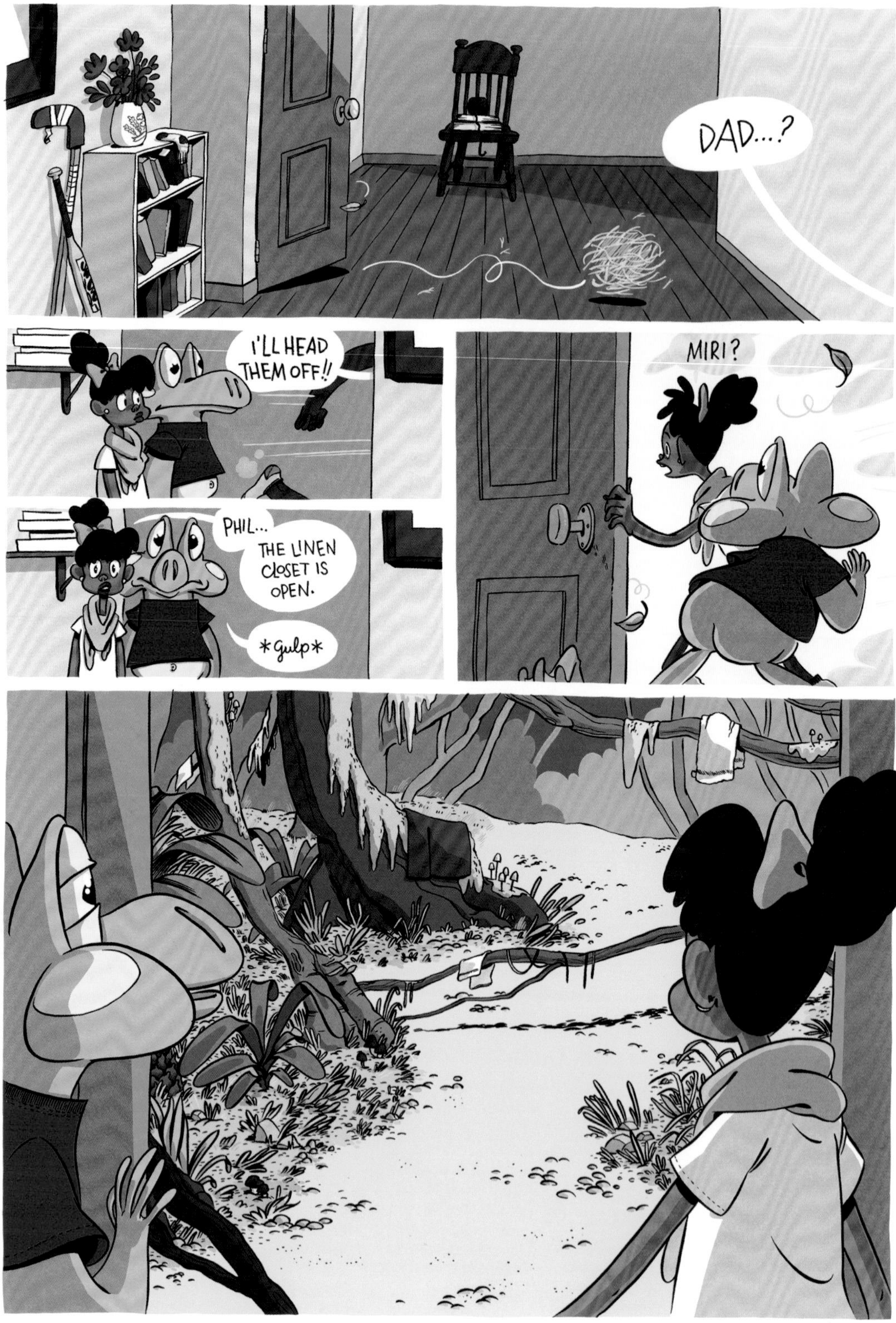
DAD...?
I'LL HEAD THEM OFF!!
PHIL...
THE LINEN CLOSET IS OPEN.
gulp
MIRI?

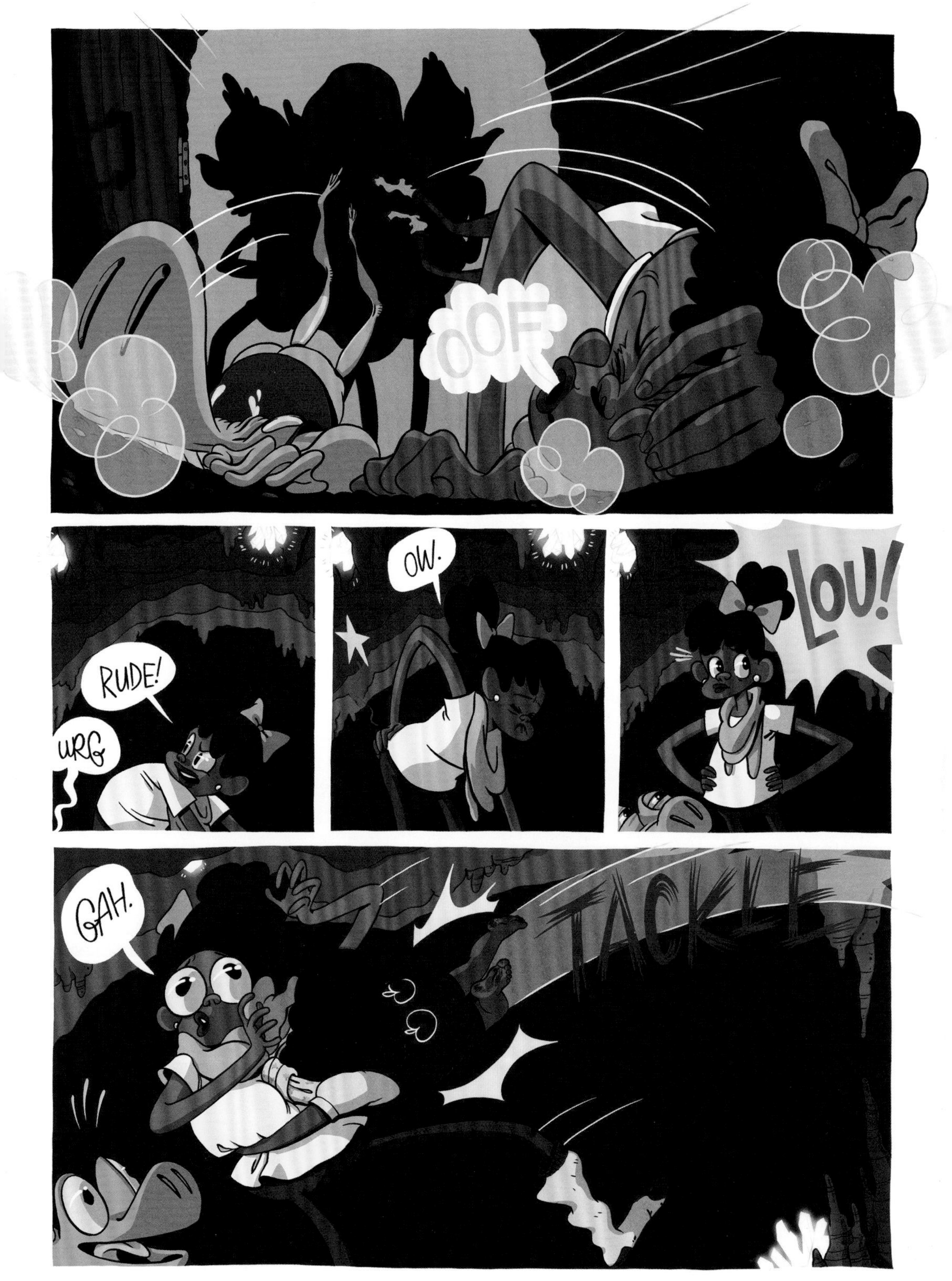
OOF
RUDE!
URG
OW.
LOU!
GAH.
TACKLE

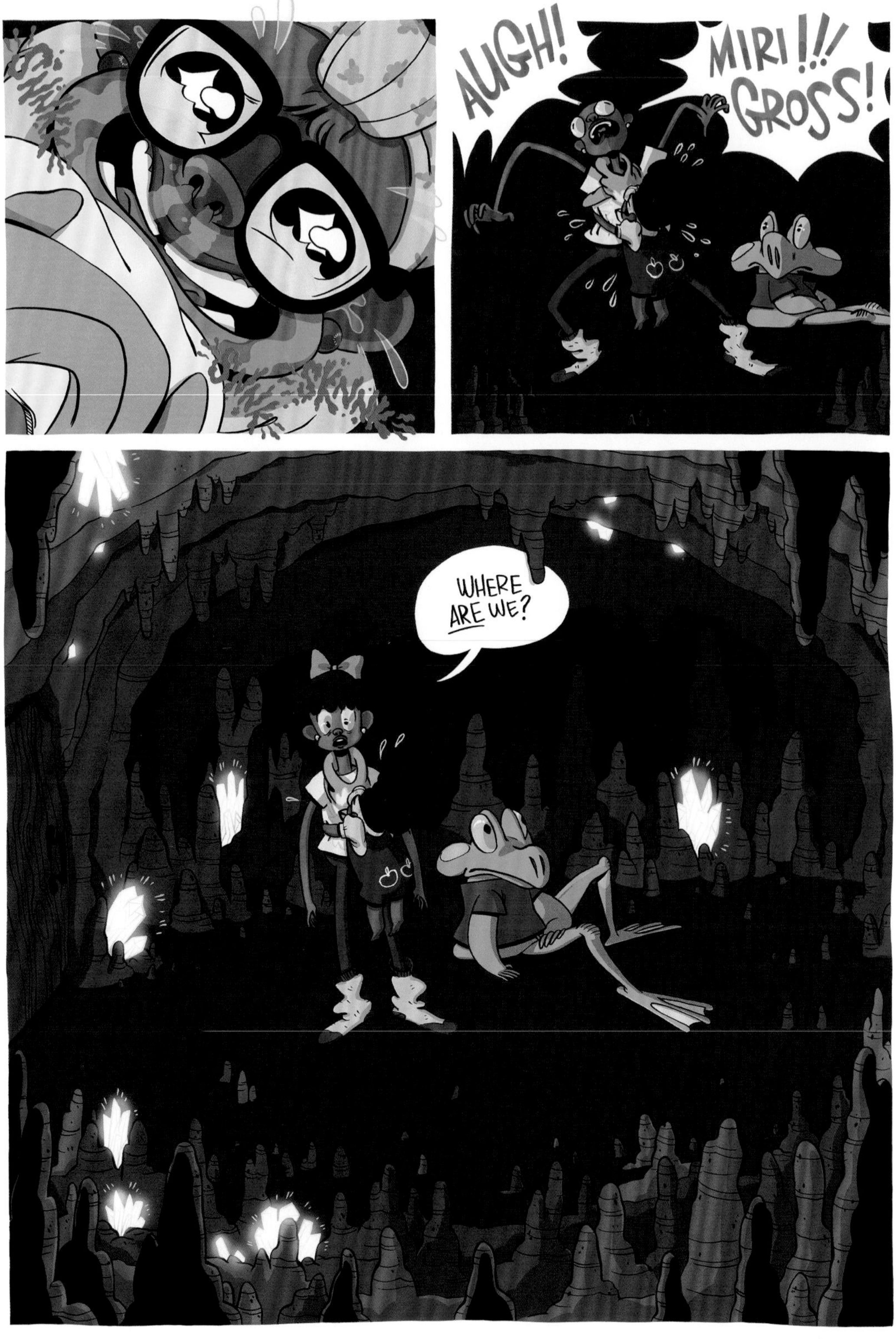
AUGH!
MIRI!!! GROSS!
WHERE ARE WE?

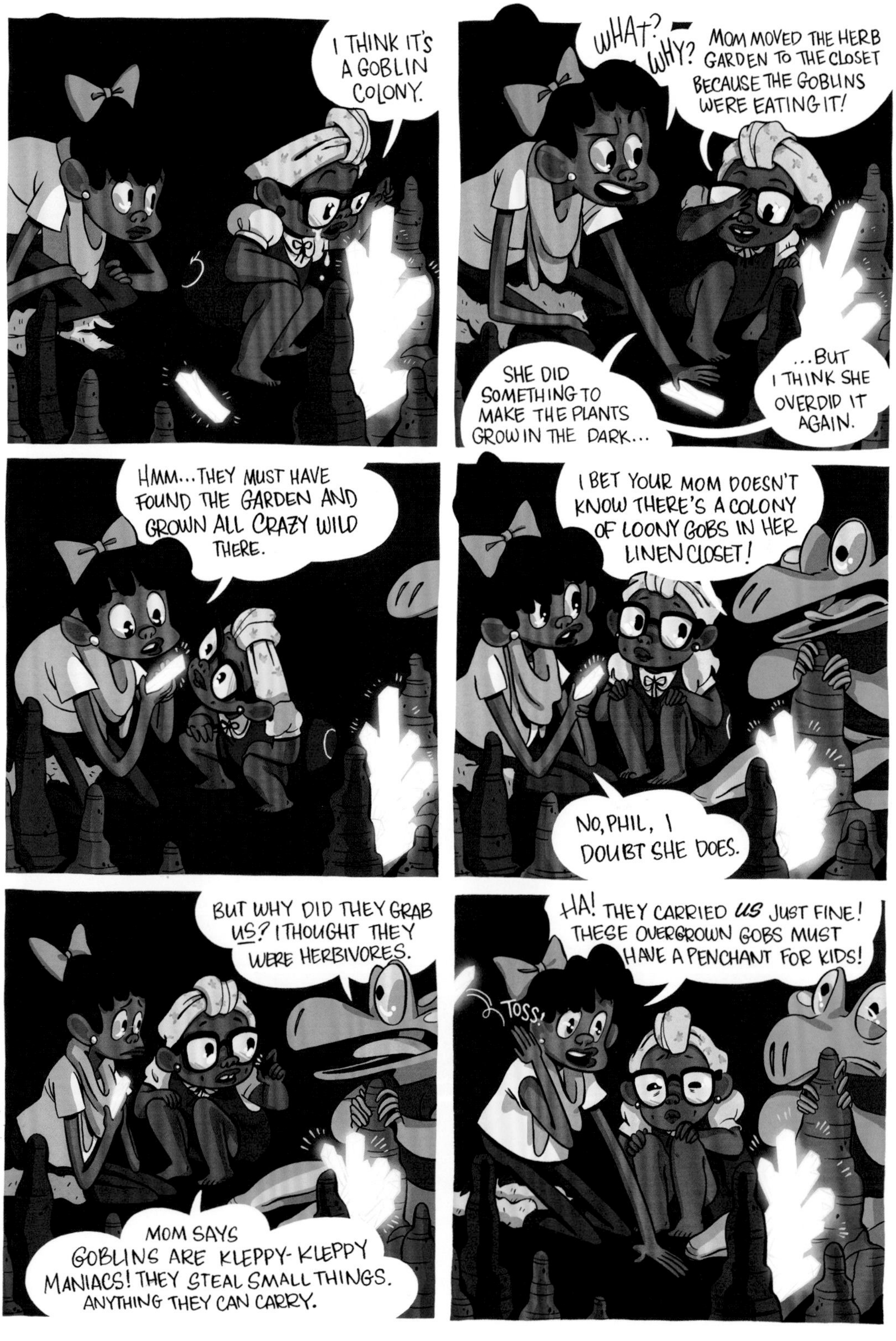
I THINK IT'S A GOBLIN COLONY.
WHAT? WHY?
MOM MOVED THE HERB GARDEN TO THE CLOSET BECAUSE THE GOBLINS WERE EATING IT!
SHE DID SOMETHING TO MAKE THE PLANTS GROW IN THE DARK...
...BUT I THINK SHE OVERDID IT AGAIN.
HMM...THEY MUST HAVE FOUND THE GARDEN AND GROWN ALL CRAZY WILD THERE.
I BET YOUR MOM DOESN'T KNOW THERE'S A COLONY OF LOONY GOBS IN HER LINEN CLOSET!
NO, PHIL, I DOUBT SHE DOES.
BUT WHY DID THEY GRAB US? I THOUGHT THEY WERE HERBIVORES.
MOM SAYS GOBLINS ARE KLEPPY-KLEPPY MANIACS! THEY STEAL SMALL THINGS. ANYTHING THEY CAN CARRY.
TOSS!
HA! THEY CARRIED US JUST FINE! THESE OVERGROWN GOBS MUST HAVE A PENCHANT FOR KIDS!

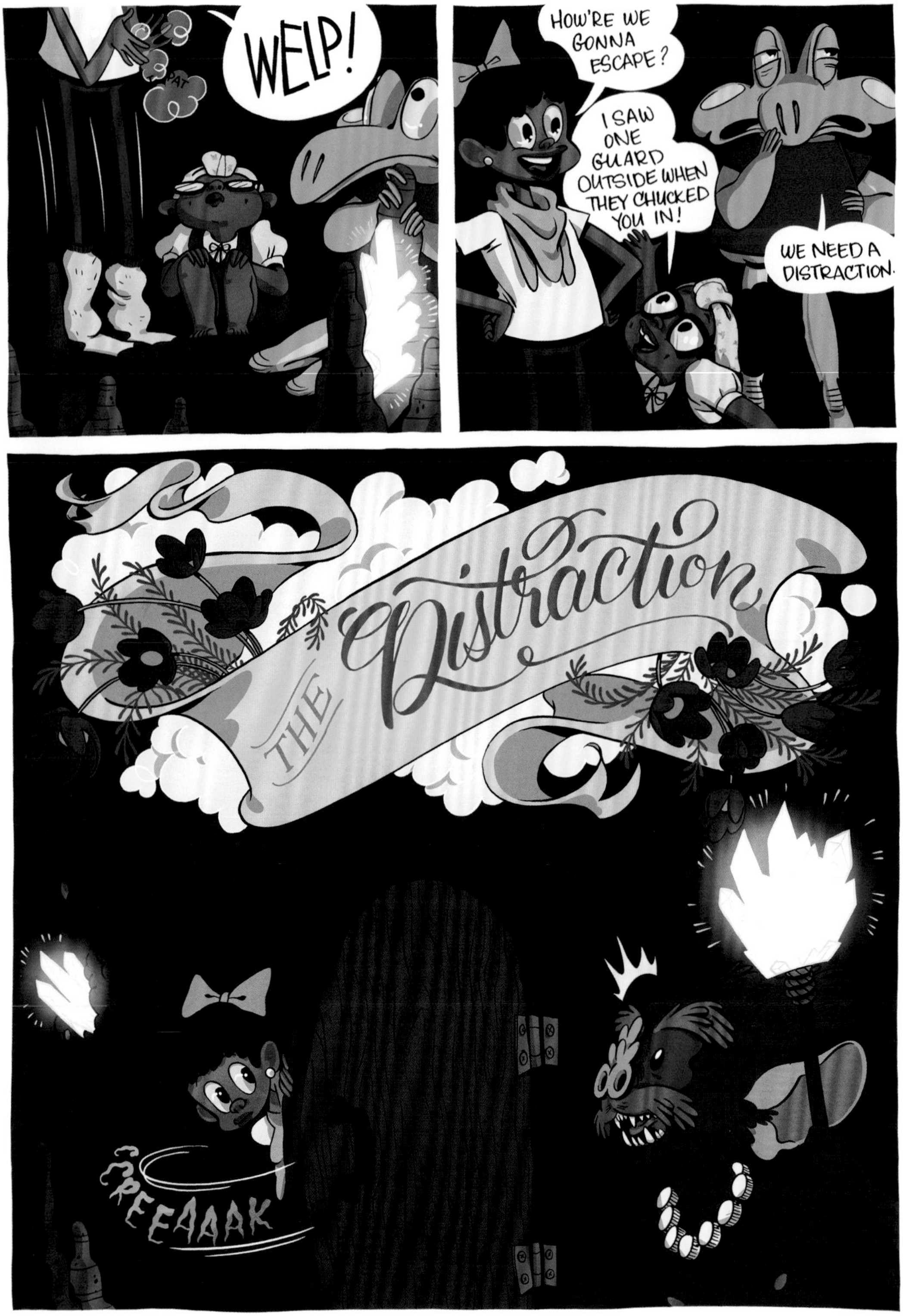

PAT
WELP!
HOW'RE WE GONNA ESCAPE?
I SAW ONE GUARD OUTSIDE WHEN THEY CHUCKED YOU IN!
WE NEED A DISTRACTION.
THE Distraction
CREEAAAK

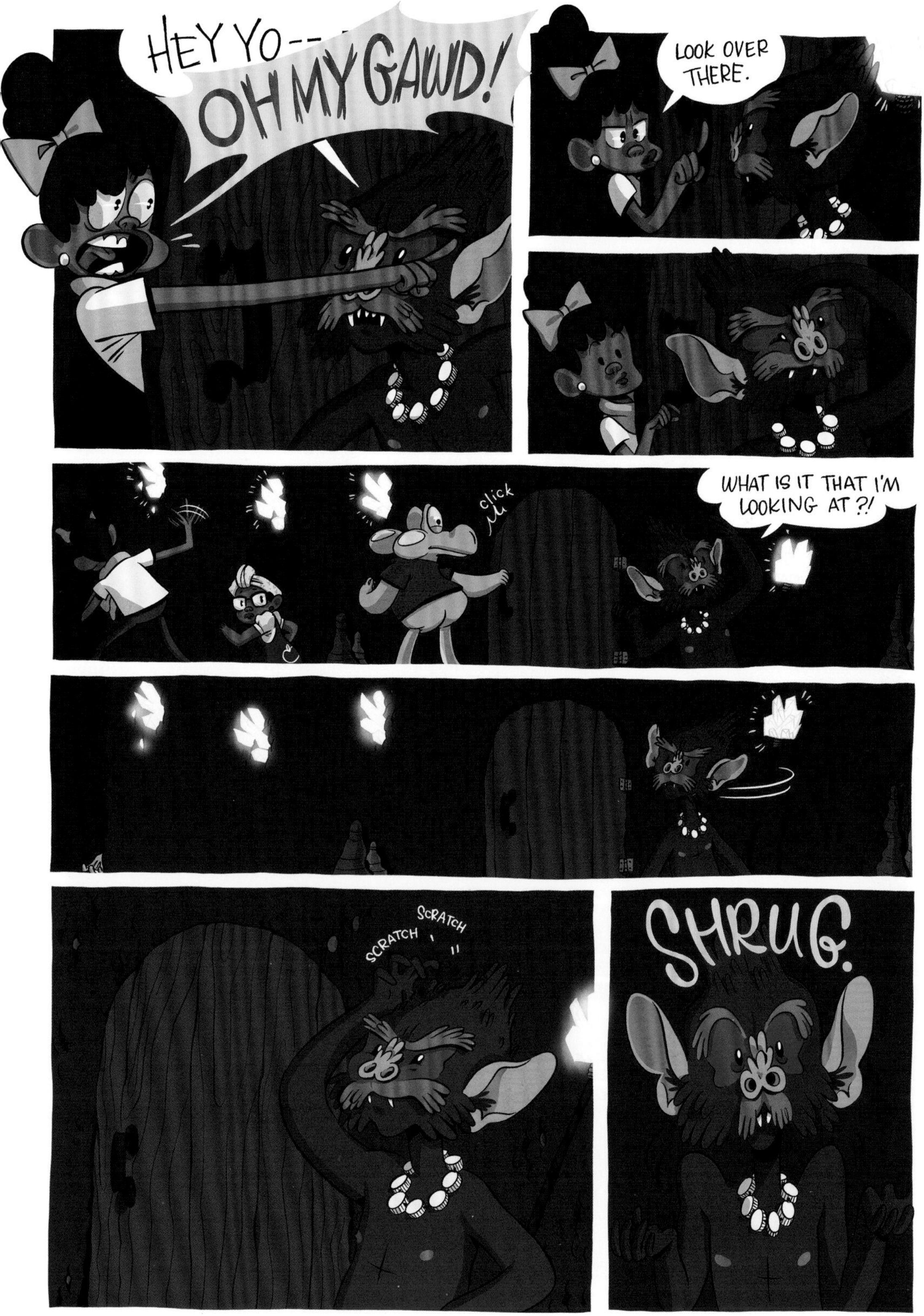
HEY YO--
OH MY GAWD!
LOOK OVER THERE.
click
WHAT IS IT THAT I'M LOOKING AT ?!
SCRATCH SCRATCH
SHRUG.

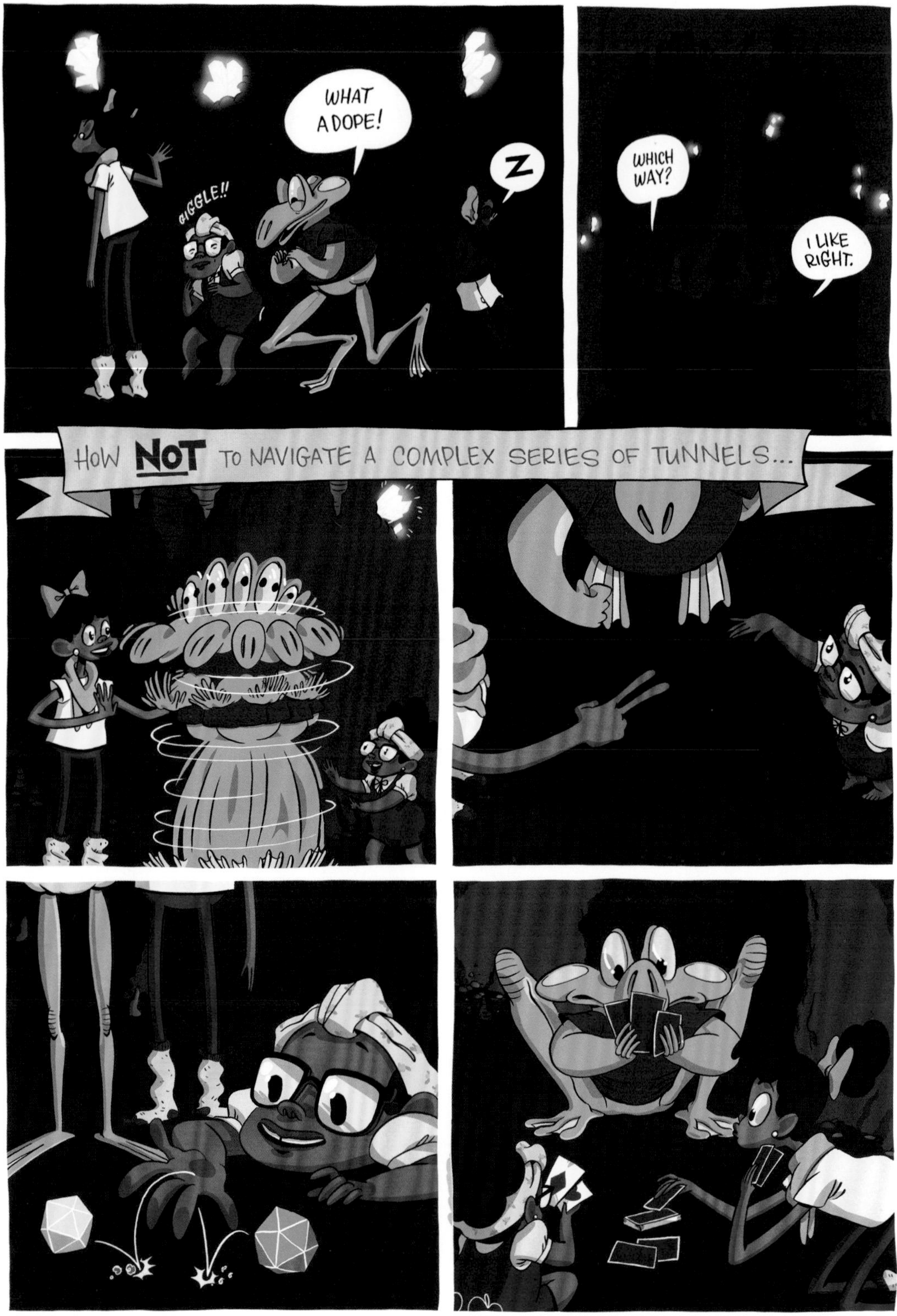
WHAT A DOPE!
GIGGLE!!
Z
WHICH WAY?
I LIKE RIGHT.
HOW NOT TO NAVIGATE A COMPLEX SERIES OF TUNNELS...

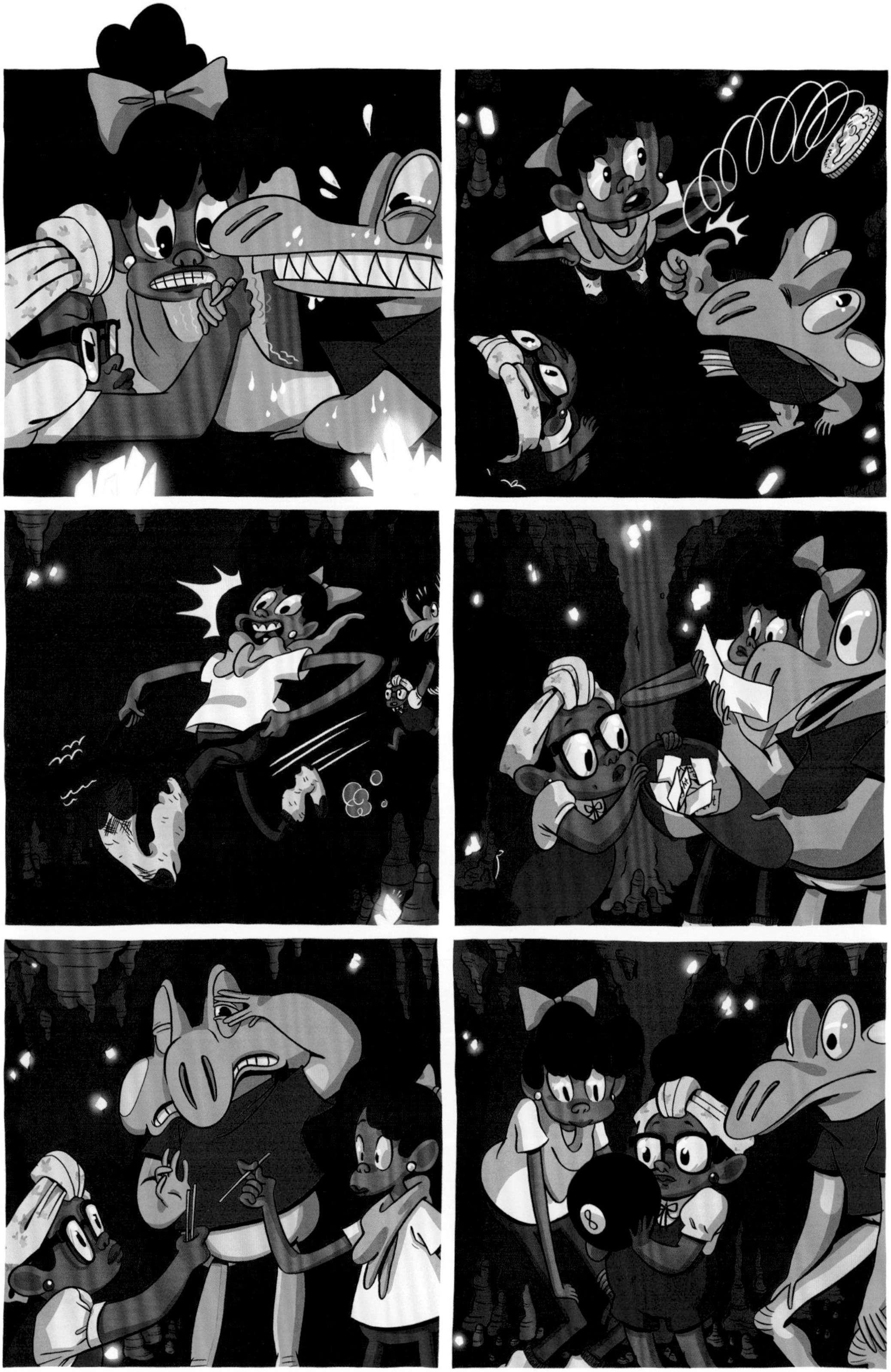

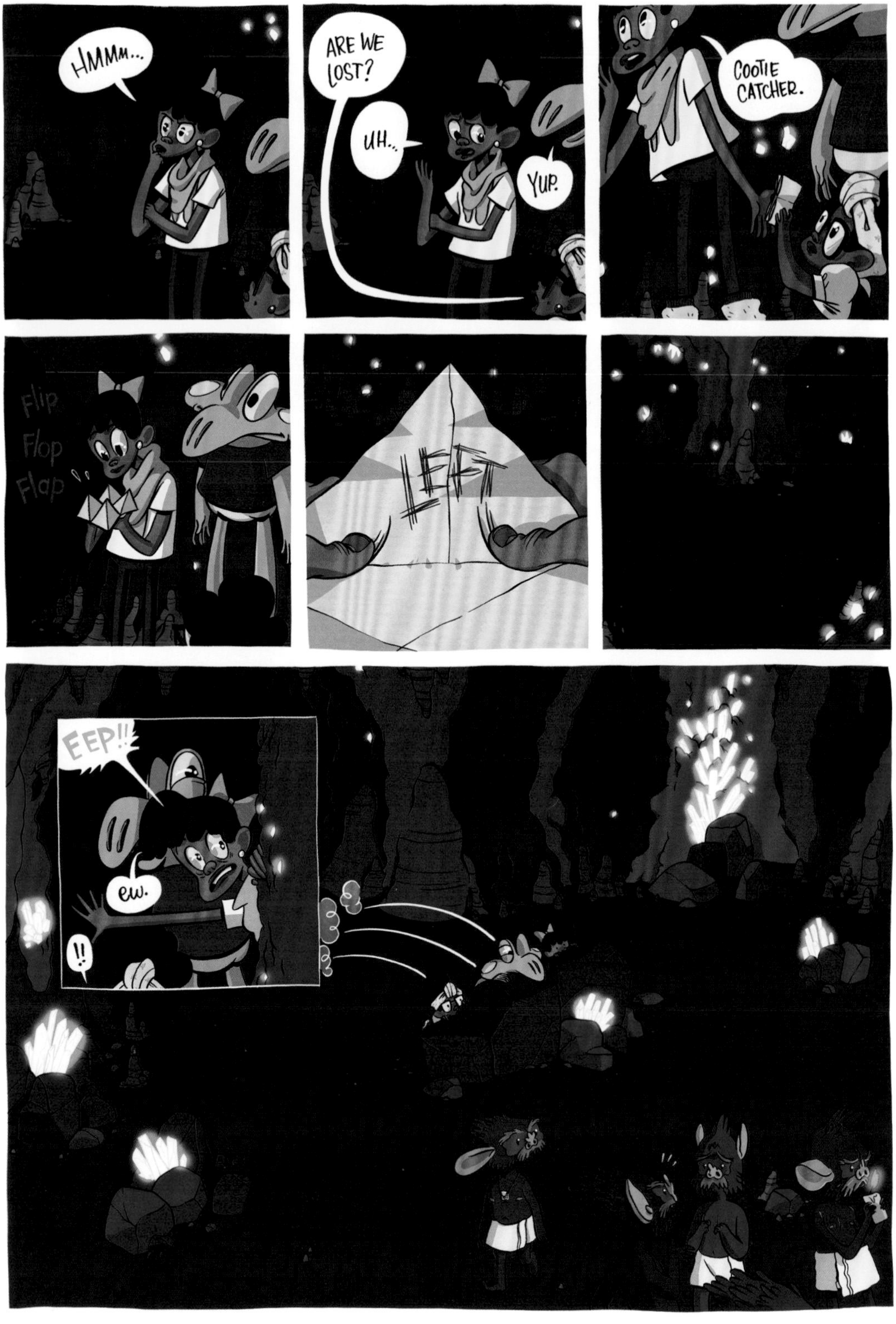
HMMM...
ARE WE LOST?
UH...
YUP.
COOTIE CATCHER.
Flip
Flop
Flap
LEFT
EEP!!
ew.
!!

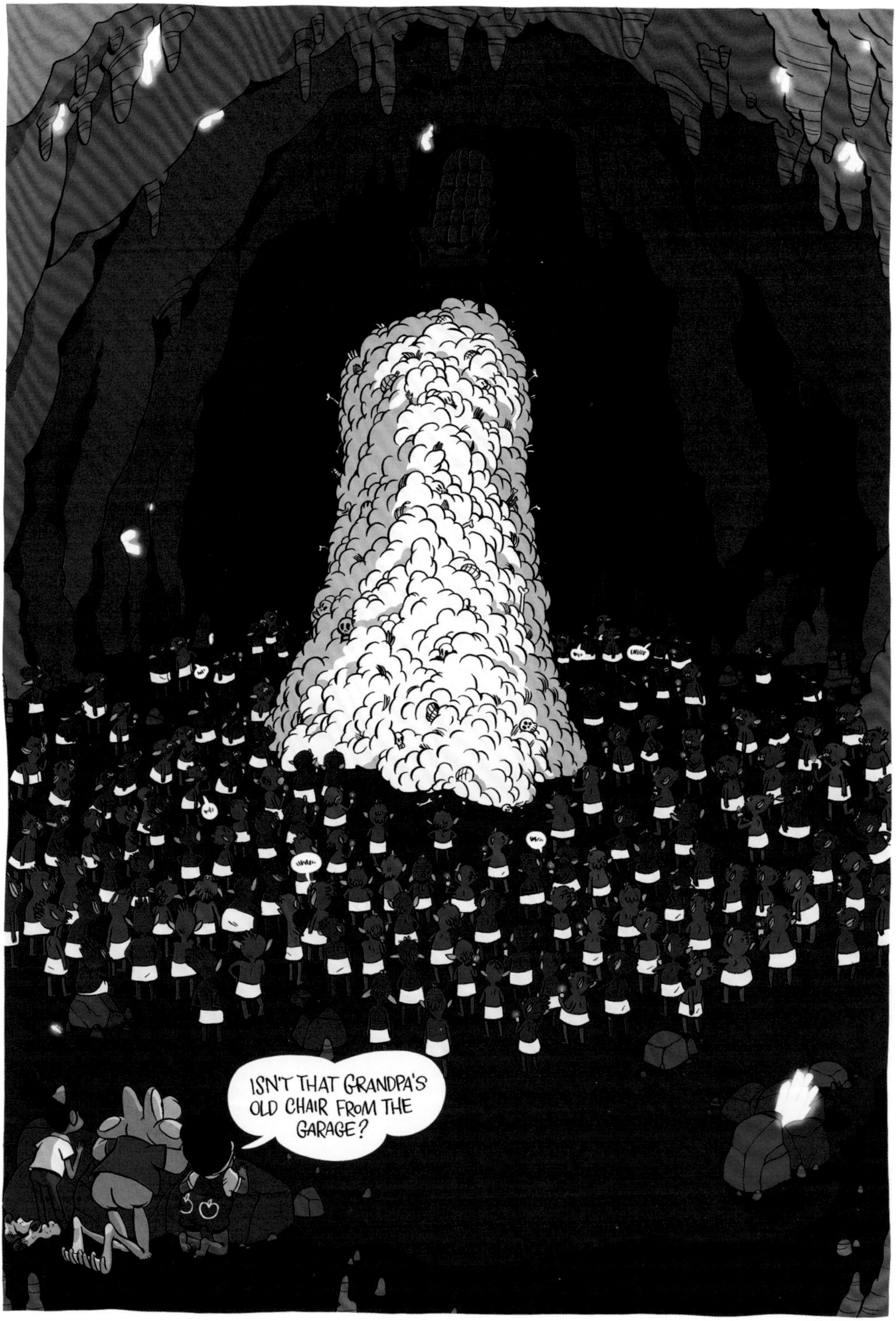
ISN'T THAT GRANDPA'S OLD CHAIR FROM THE GARAGE?

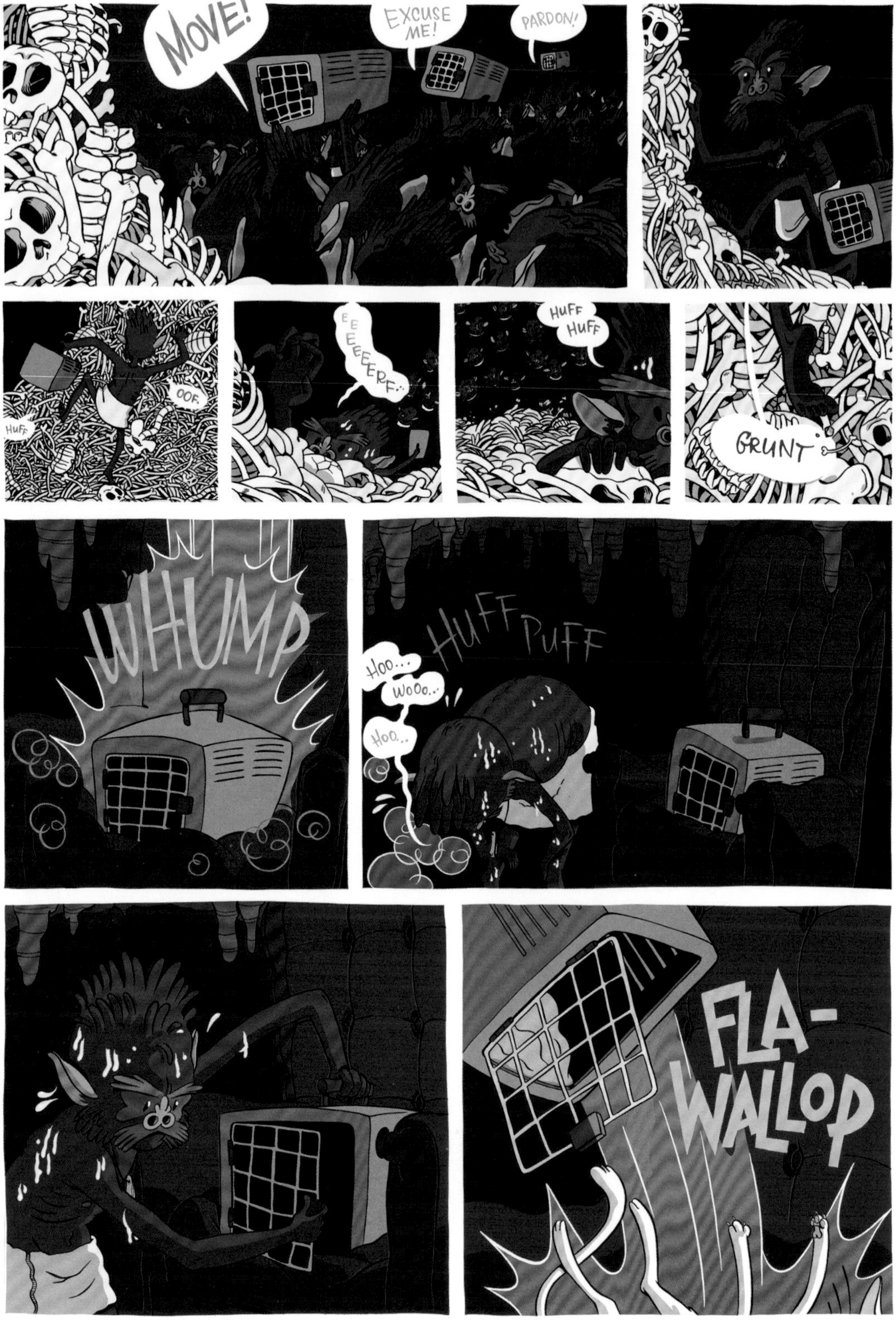
MOVE!
EXCUSE ME!
PARDON!
OOF.
HUFF
EEEEEERF...
HUFF HUFF
GRUNT
WHUMP
HUFF PUFF
Hoo...
wooo...
Hoo...
FLA-WALLOP

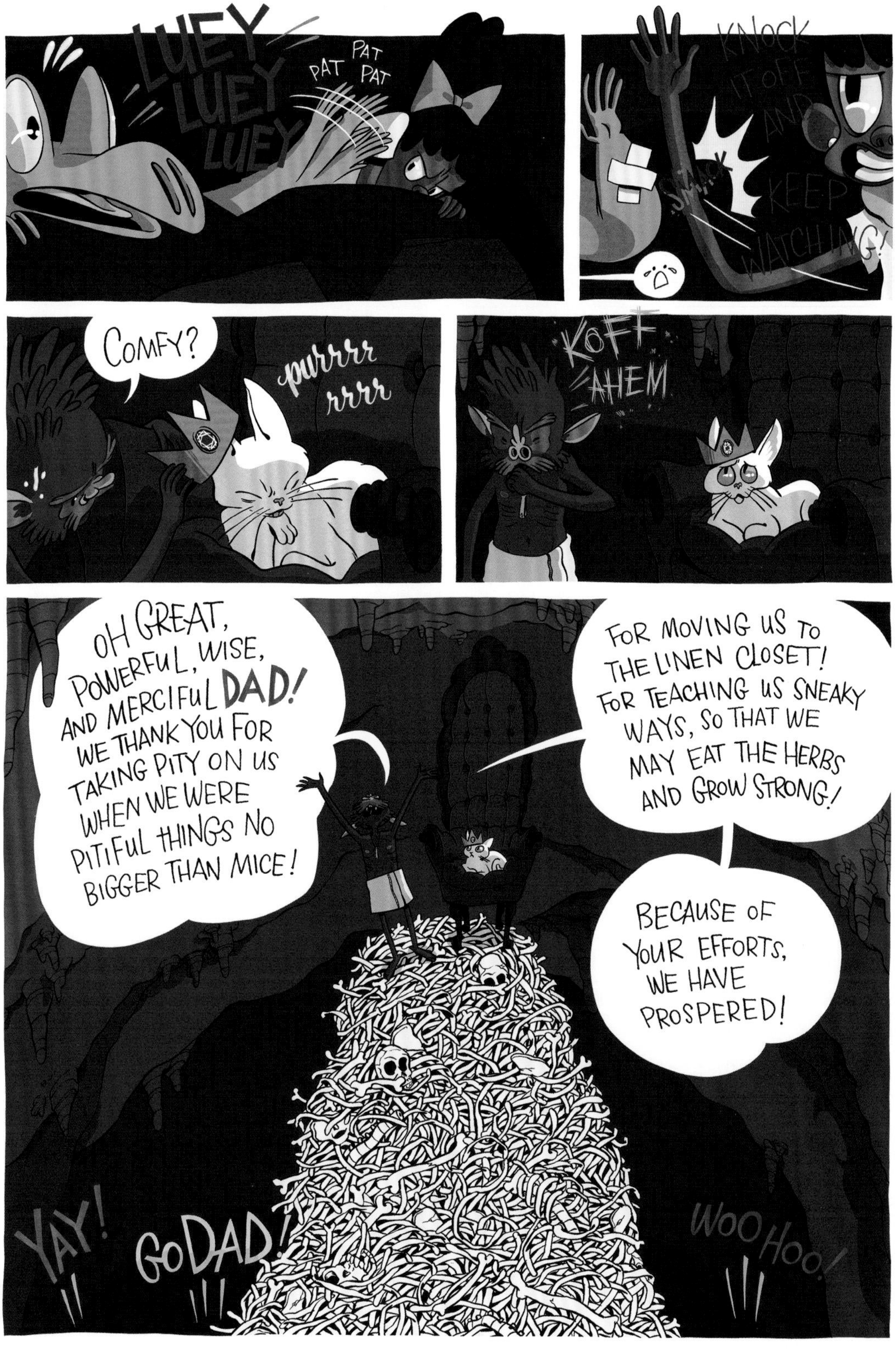
LUEY LUEY LUEY
PAT PAT PAT
KNOCK IT OFF AND KEEP WATCHING!
SMACK
COMFY?
purrrr rrrr
KOFF AHEM
OH GREAT, POWERFUL, WISE, AND MERCIFUL DAD! WE THANK YOU FOR TAKING PITY ON US WHEN WE WERE PITIFUL THINGS NO BIGGER THAN MICE!
FOR MOVING US TO THE LINEN CLOSET! FOR TEACHING US SNEAKY WAYS, SO THAT WE MAY EAT THE HERBS AND GROW STRONG!
BECAUSE OF YOUR EFFORTS, WE HAVE PROSPERED!
YAY!
GO DAD!
WOO HOO!

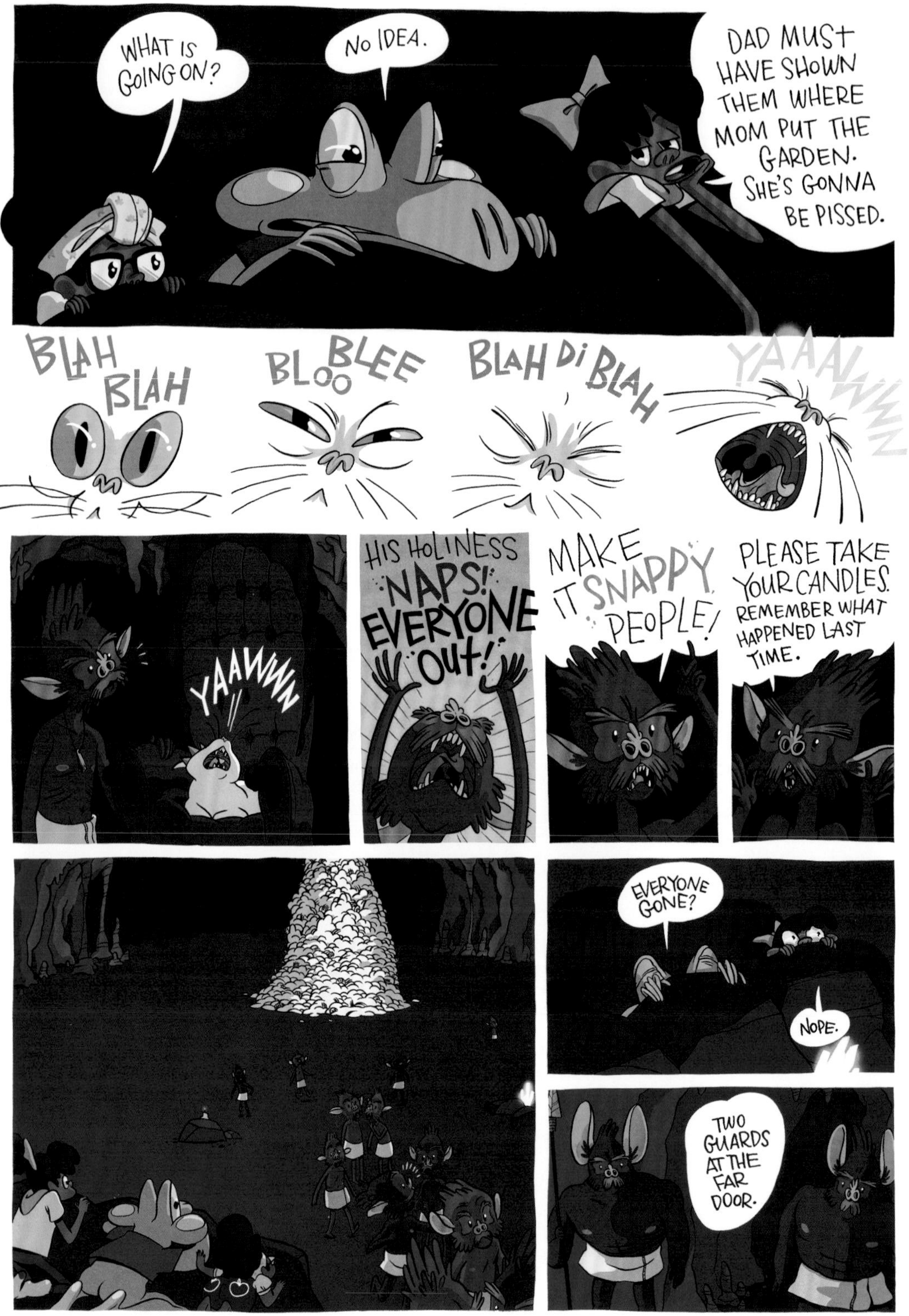
WHAT IS GOING ON?
NO IDEA.
DAD MUST HAVE SHOWN THEM WHERE MOM PUT THE GARDEN. SHE'S GONNA BE PISSED.
BLAH BLAH
BLOO BLEE
BLAH DI BLAH
YAAAWWN
YAAWWN
HIS HOLINESS NAPS! EVERYONE OUT!
MAKE IT SNAPPY, PEOPLE!
PLEASE TAKE YOUR CANDLES. REMEMBER WHAT HAPPENED LAST TIME.
EVERYONE GONE?
NOPE.
TWO GUARDS AT THE FAR DOOR.

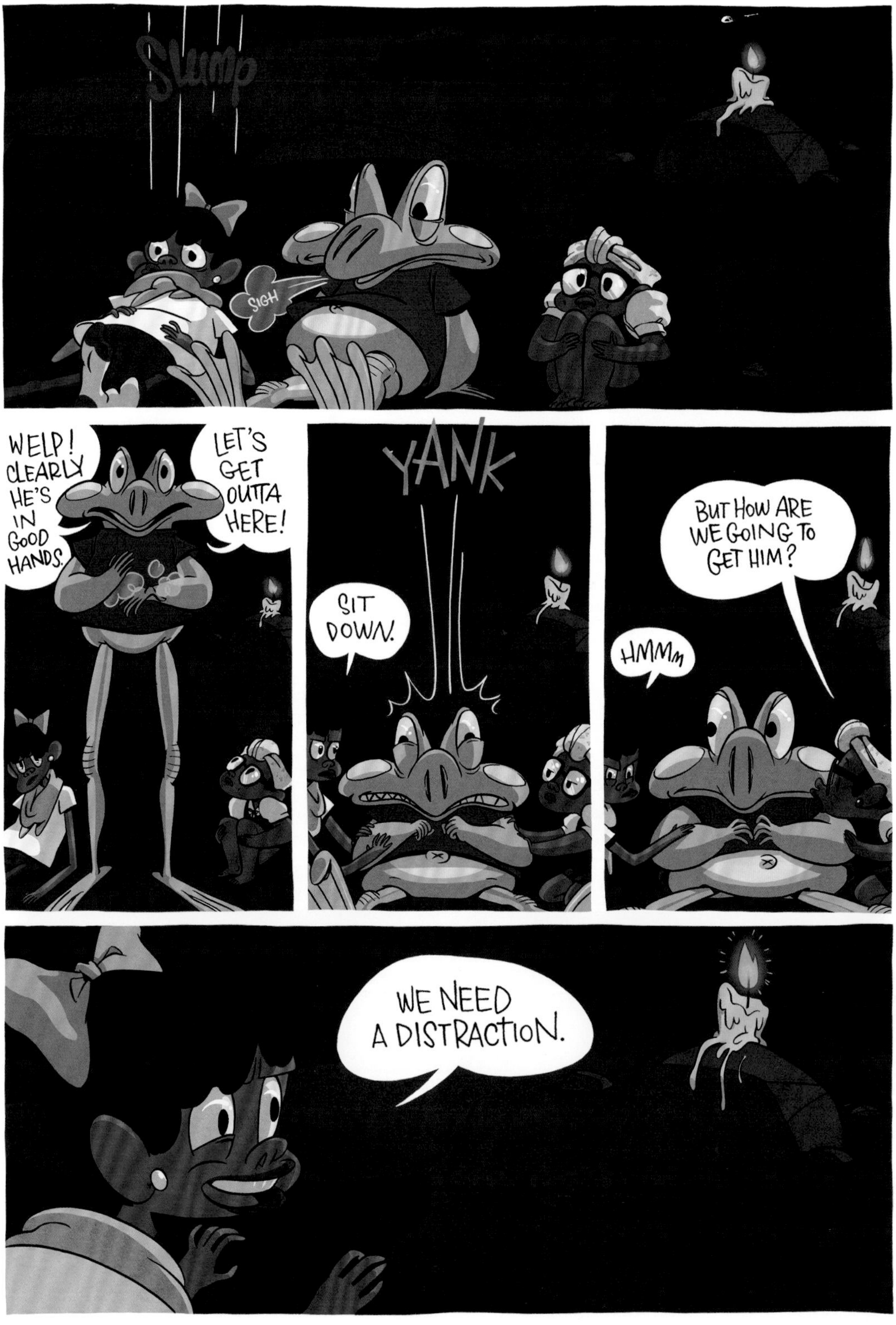
SLUMP
SIGH
WELP! CLEARLY HE'S IN GOOD HANDS.
LET'S GET OUTTA HERE!
YANK
SIT DOWN.
BUT HOW ARE WE GOING TO GET HIM?
HMMm
WE NEED A DISTRACTION.

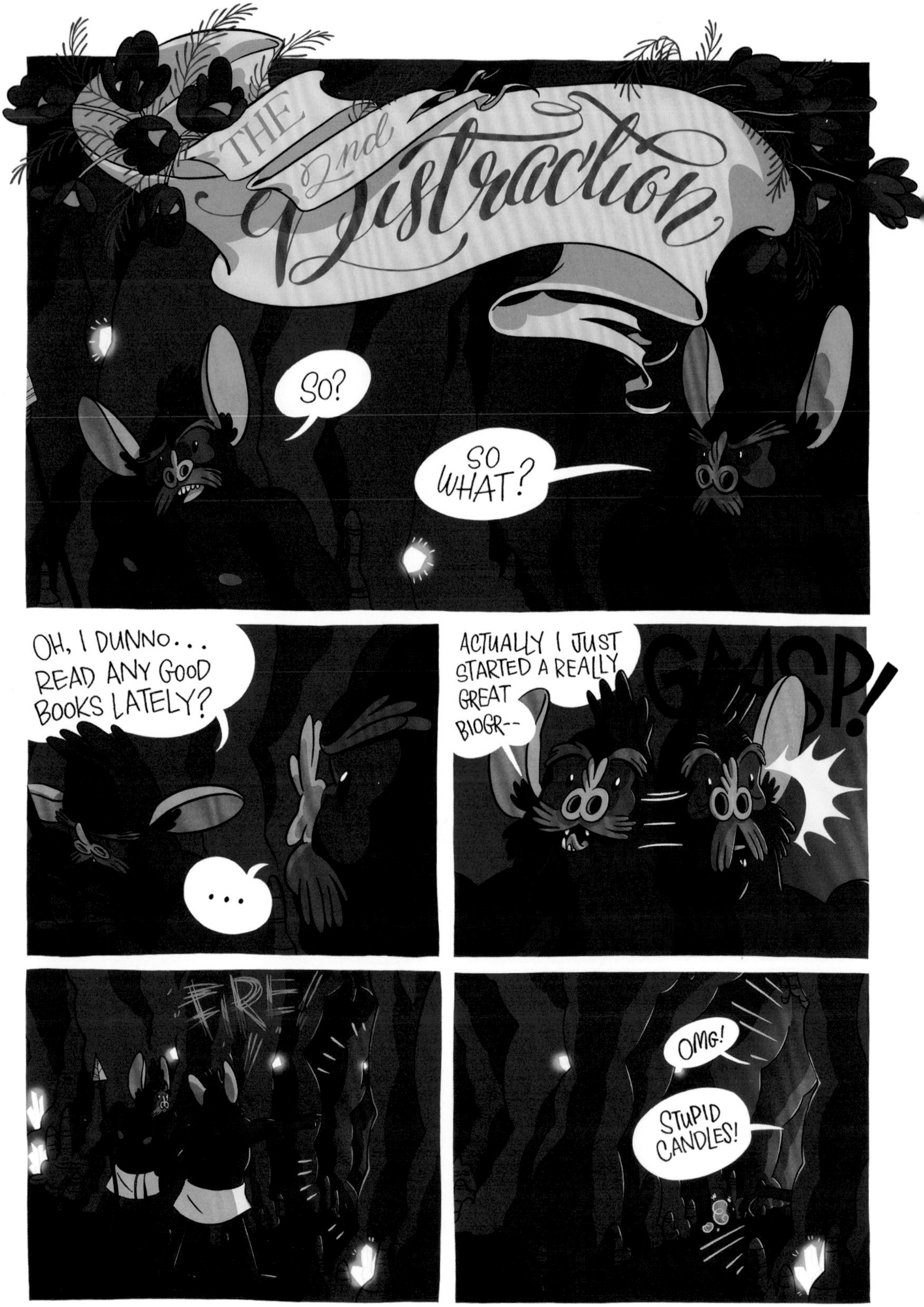
THE 2nd Distraction
SO?
SO WHAT?
OH, I DUNNO... READ ANY GOOD BOOKS LATELY?
...
ACTUALLY I JUST STARTED A REALLY GREAT BIOGR--
GASP!
FIRE!
OMG!
STUPID CANDLES!

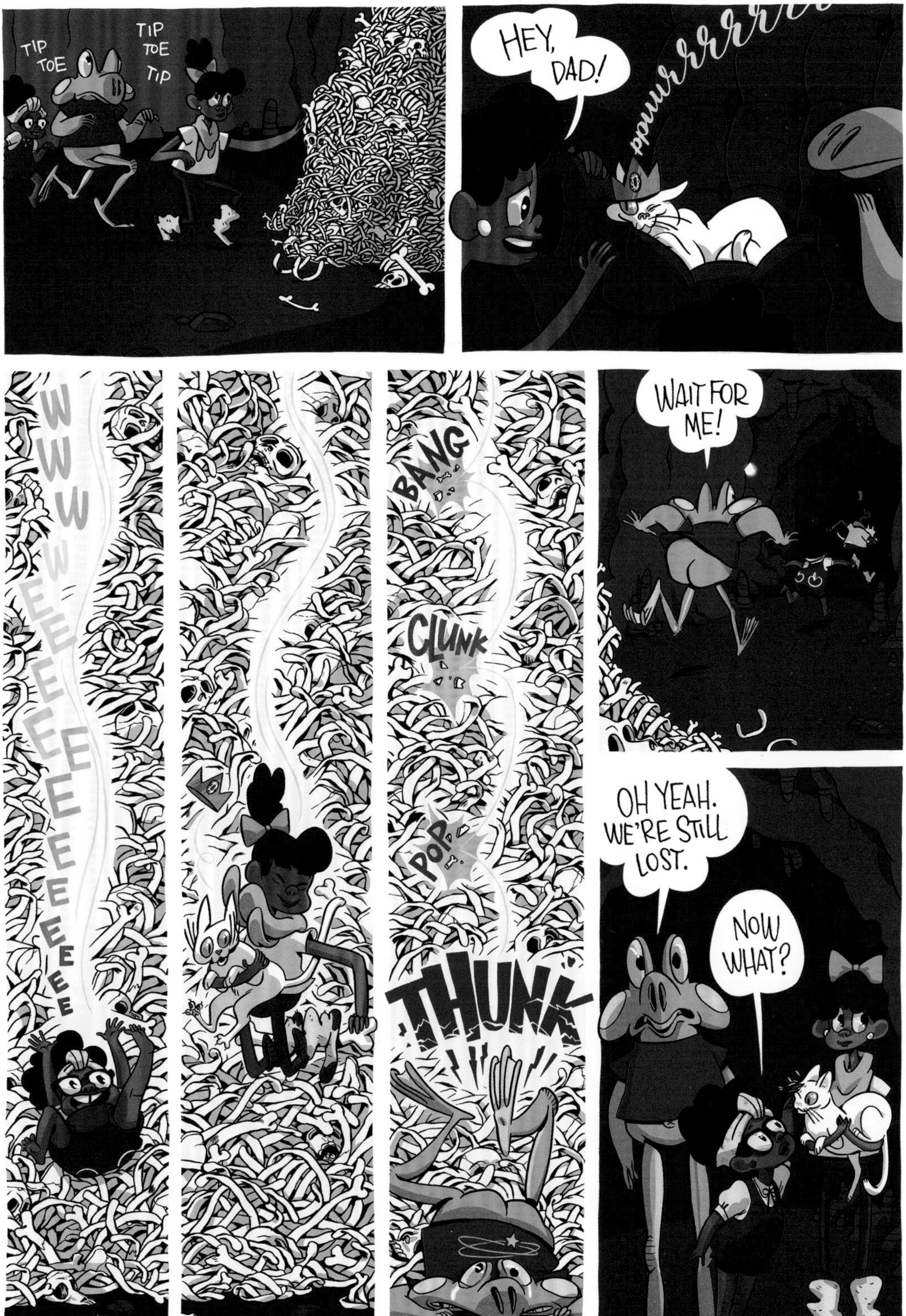
TIP TOE
TIP TOE TIP
HEY, DAD!
purrrrrrrrr
WWWWWEEEEEEEEEEEEE
BANG
CLUNK
POP
THUNK
WAIT FOR ME!
OH YEAH. WE'RE STILL LOST.
NOW WHAT?

MIRI!!
ZOOM
WAIT!
NO, PHIL!
GET IT, GET IT!!
GET WHAT?
SPIN
WHADJA GET?
A DUNGEON MAP!

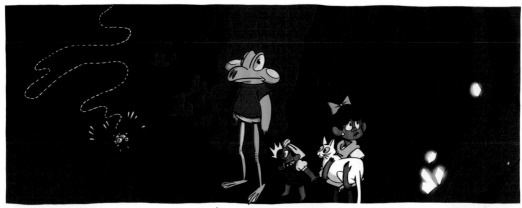

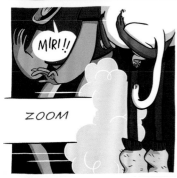

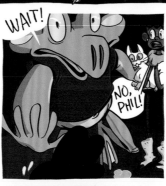

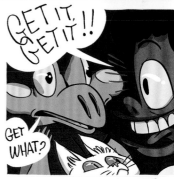

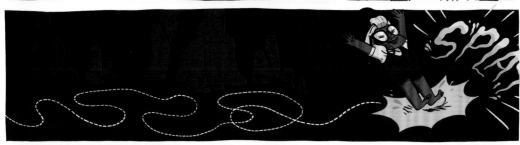

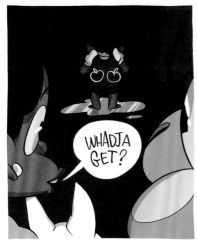

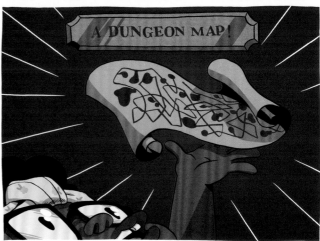

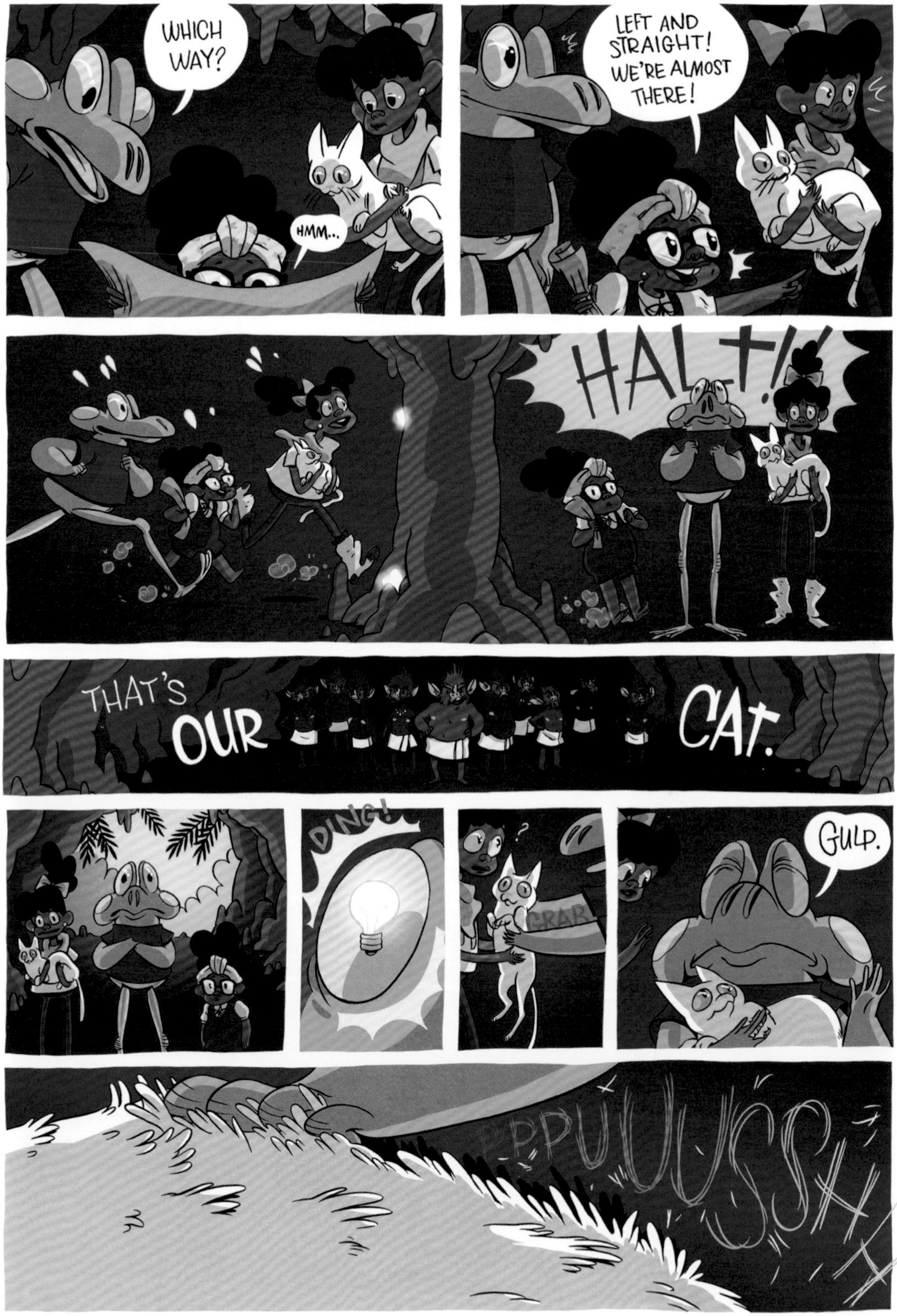
WHICH WAY?
HMM...
LEFT AND STRAIGHT! WE'RE ALMOST THERE!
HALT!!
THAT'S OUR CAT.
DING!
?
GRAB
GULP.
PPPUUUSSH

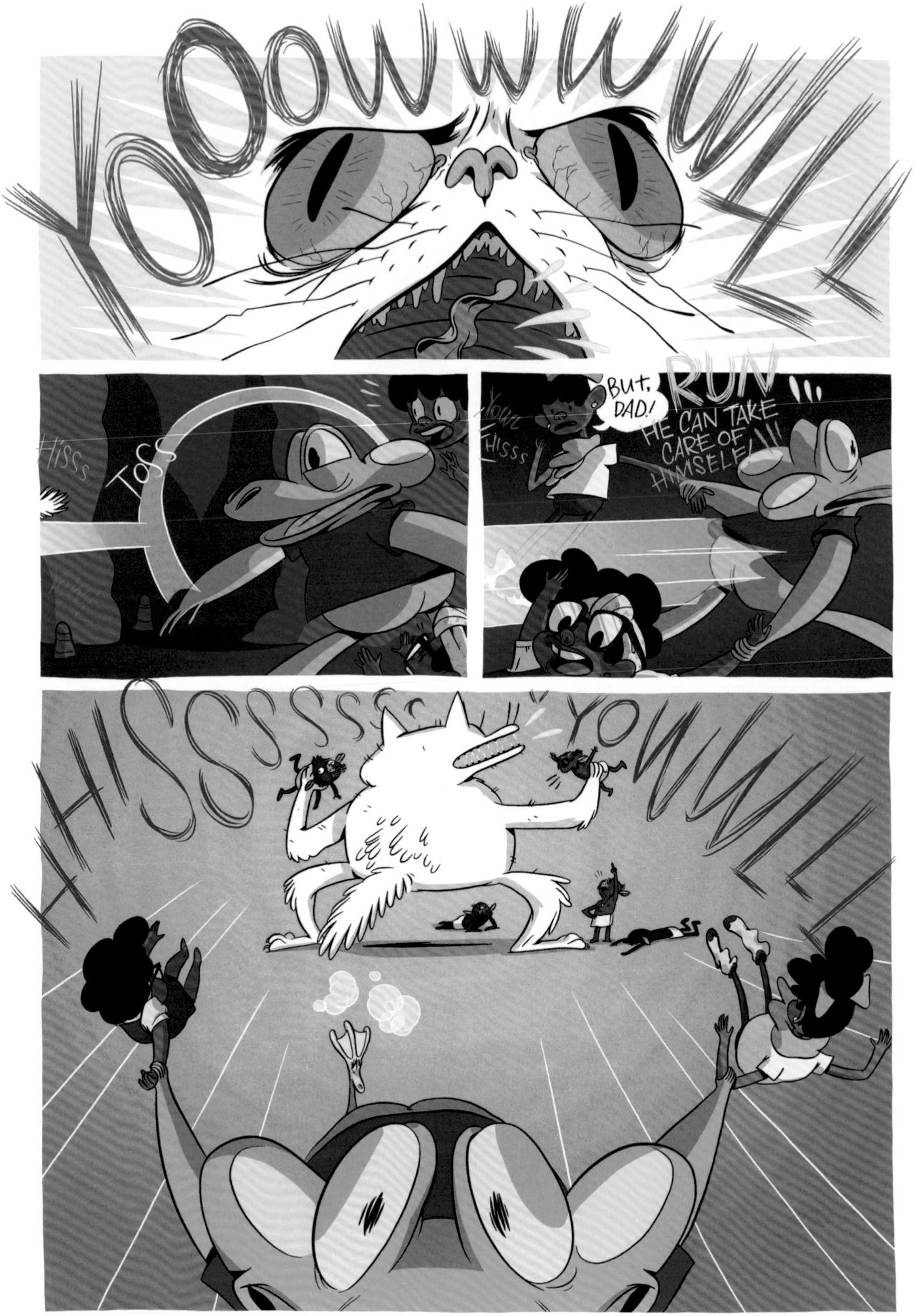
YOOOWWWWLL!!
HISSS
TOSS
YOWL
HISSS
BUT, DAD!
RUN!!
HE CAN TAKE CARE OF HIMSELF!!!
HISSSSSSS
YOWWWLL!

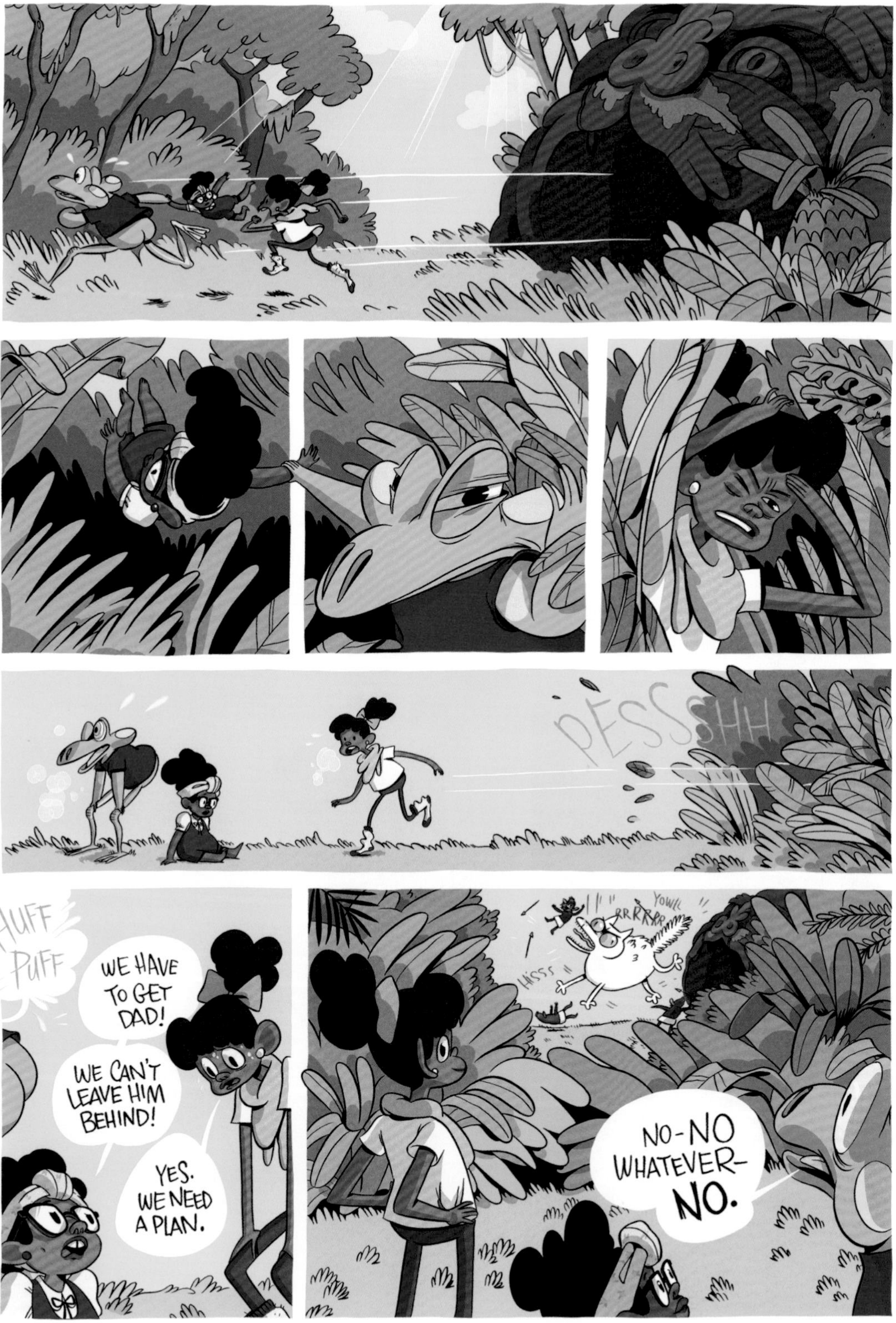
PESSSHH
HUFF PUFF
WE HAVE TO GET DAD!
WE CAN'T LEAVE HIM BEHIND!
YES. WE NEED A PLAN.
YOWL
RRRRRRR
HISSS
NO-NO WHATEVER- NO.

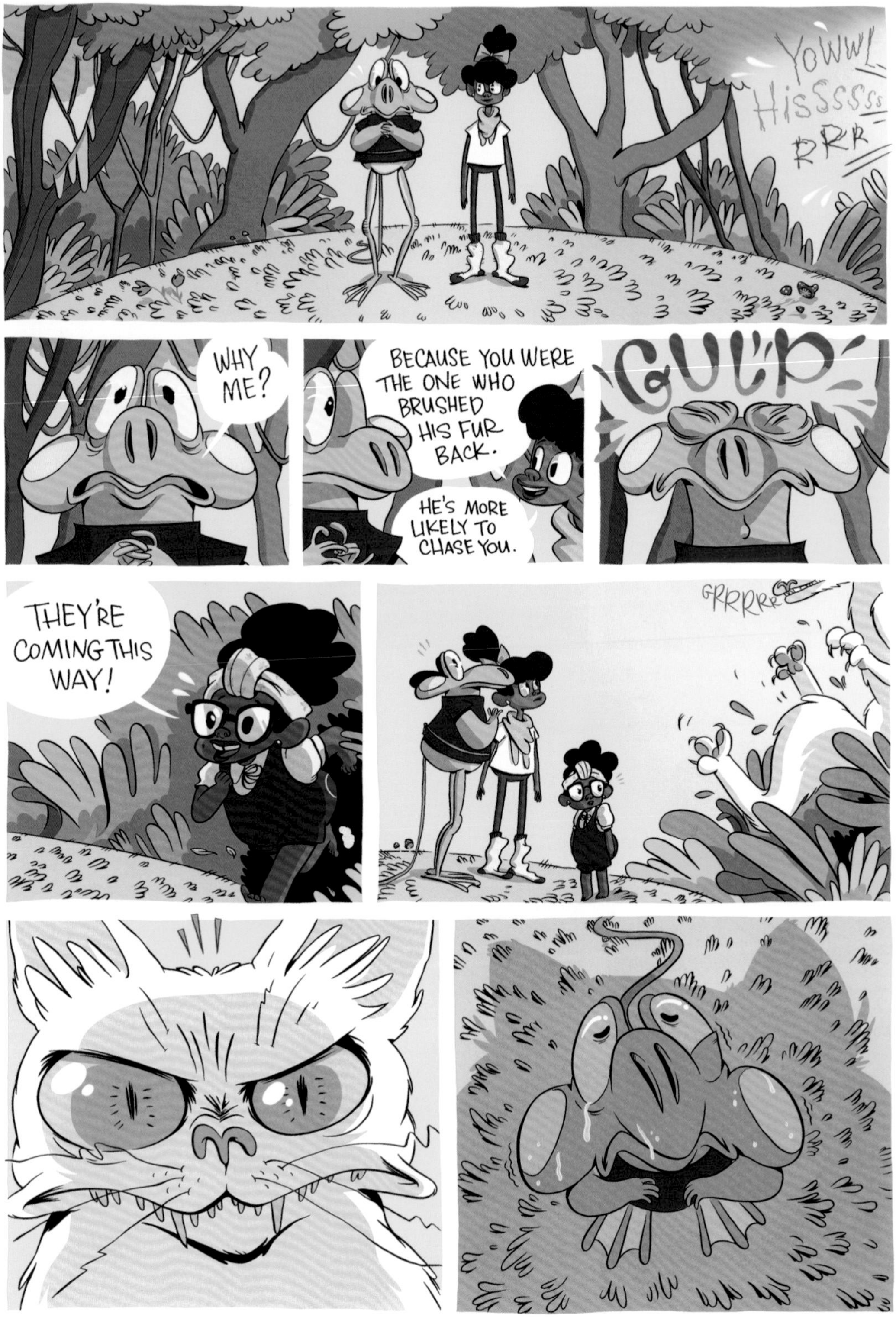
YOWWL
HISSSSSS
RRR
WHY ME?
BECAUSE YOU WERE THE ONE WHO BRUSHED HIS FUR BACK.
HE'S MORE LIKELY TO CHASE YOU.
GULP
THEY'RE COMING THIS WAY!
GRRRRR

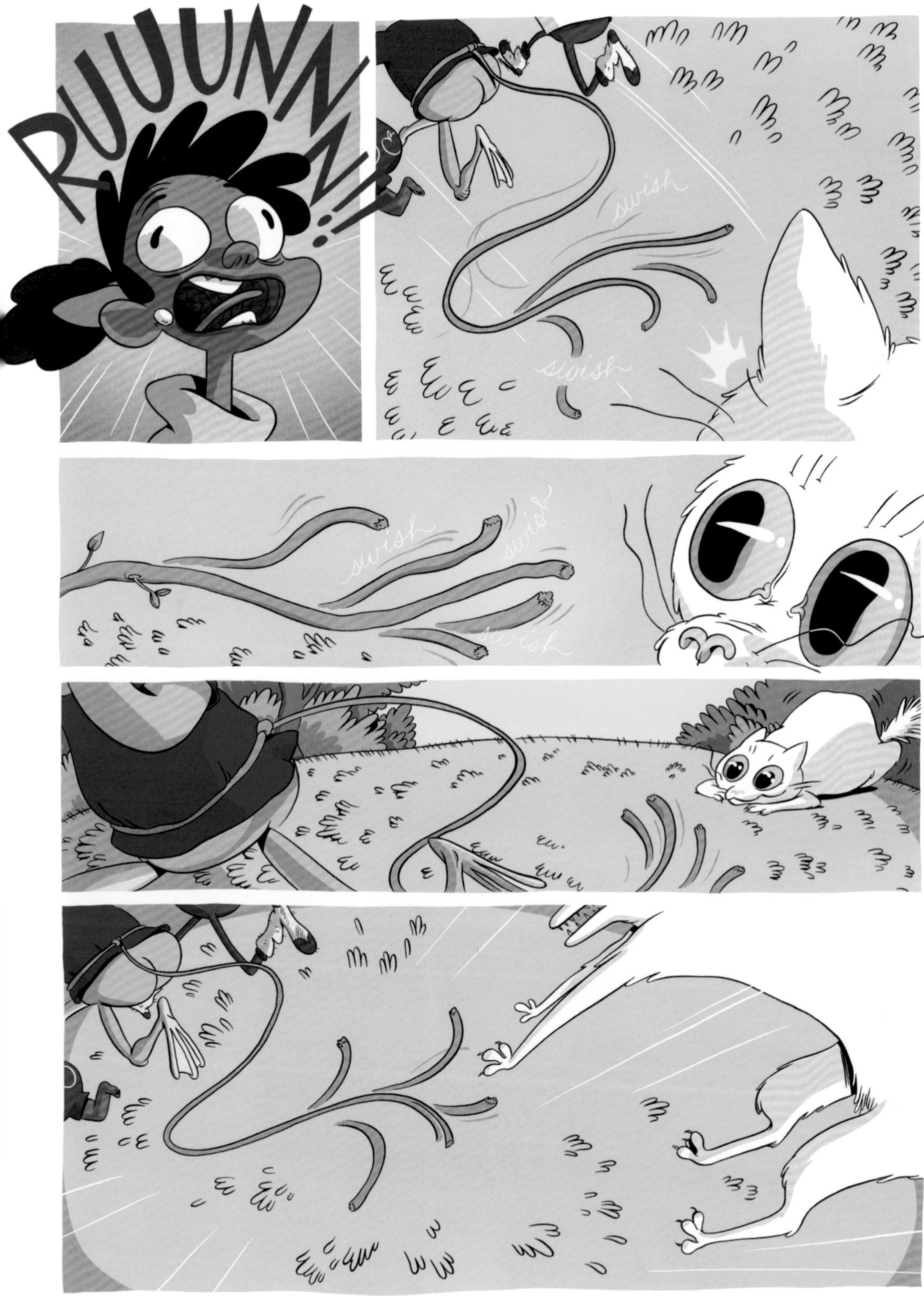
RUUUNN!!!
swish
swish
swish
swish
swish

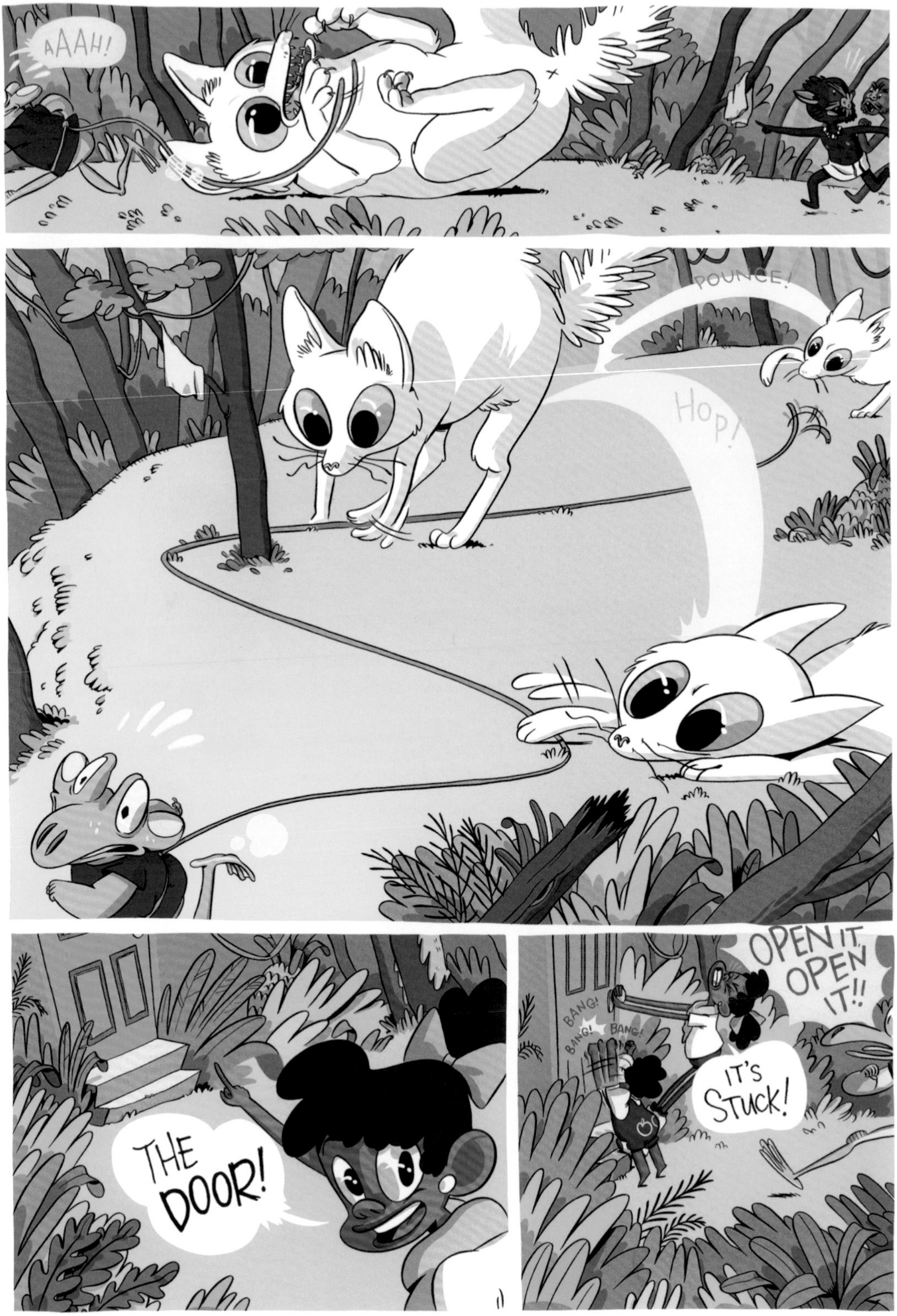
AAAH!
POUNCE!
HOP!
THE DOOR!
OPEN IT, OPEN IT!!
BANG! BANG! BANG!
IT'S STUCK!

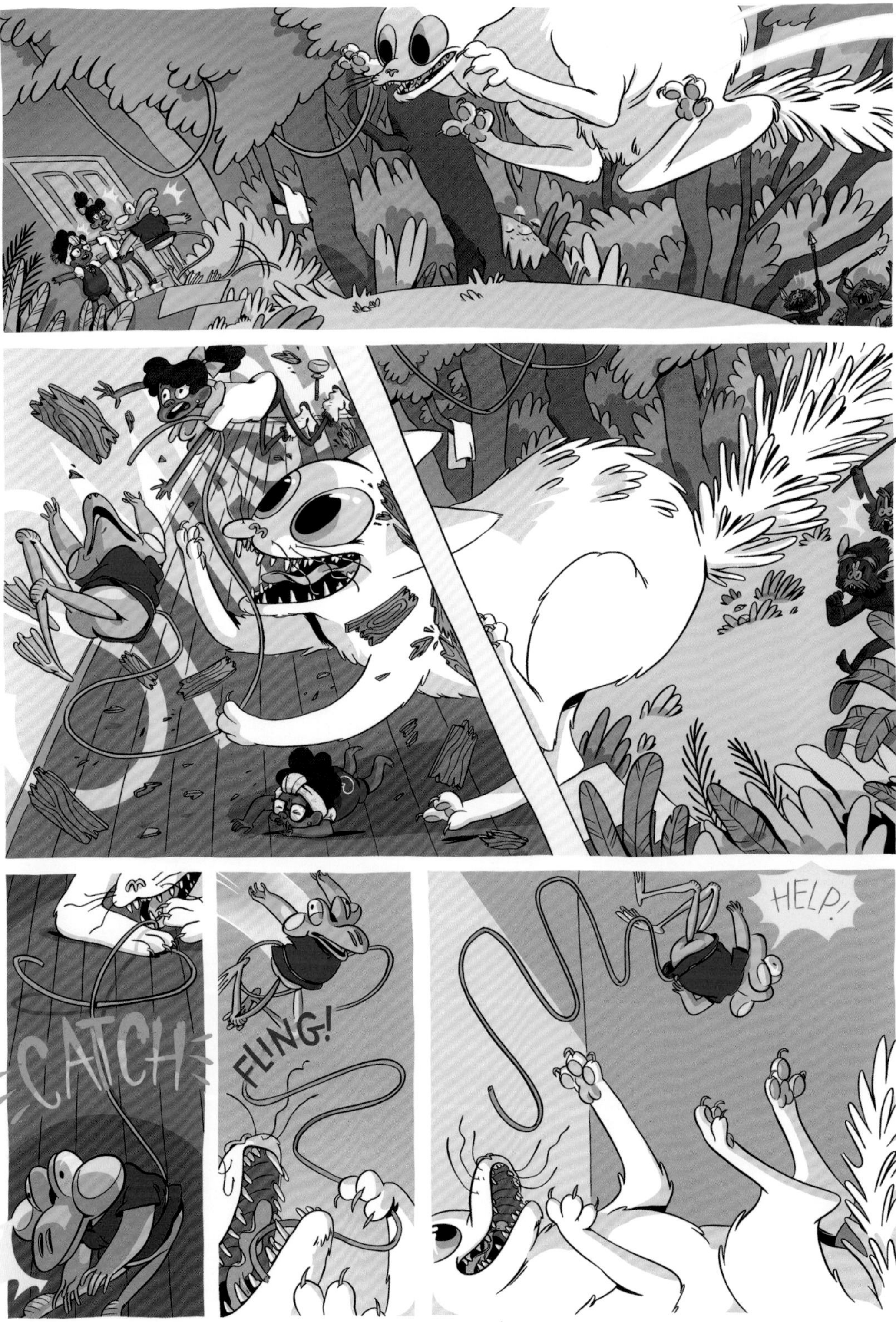
CATCH
FLING!
HELP!

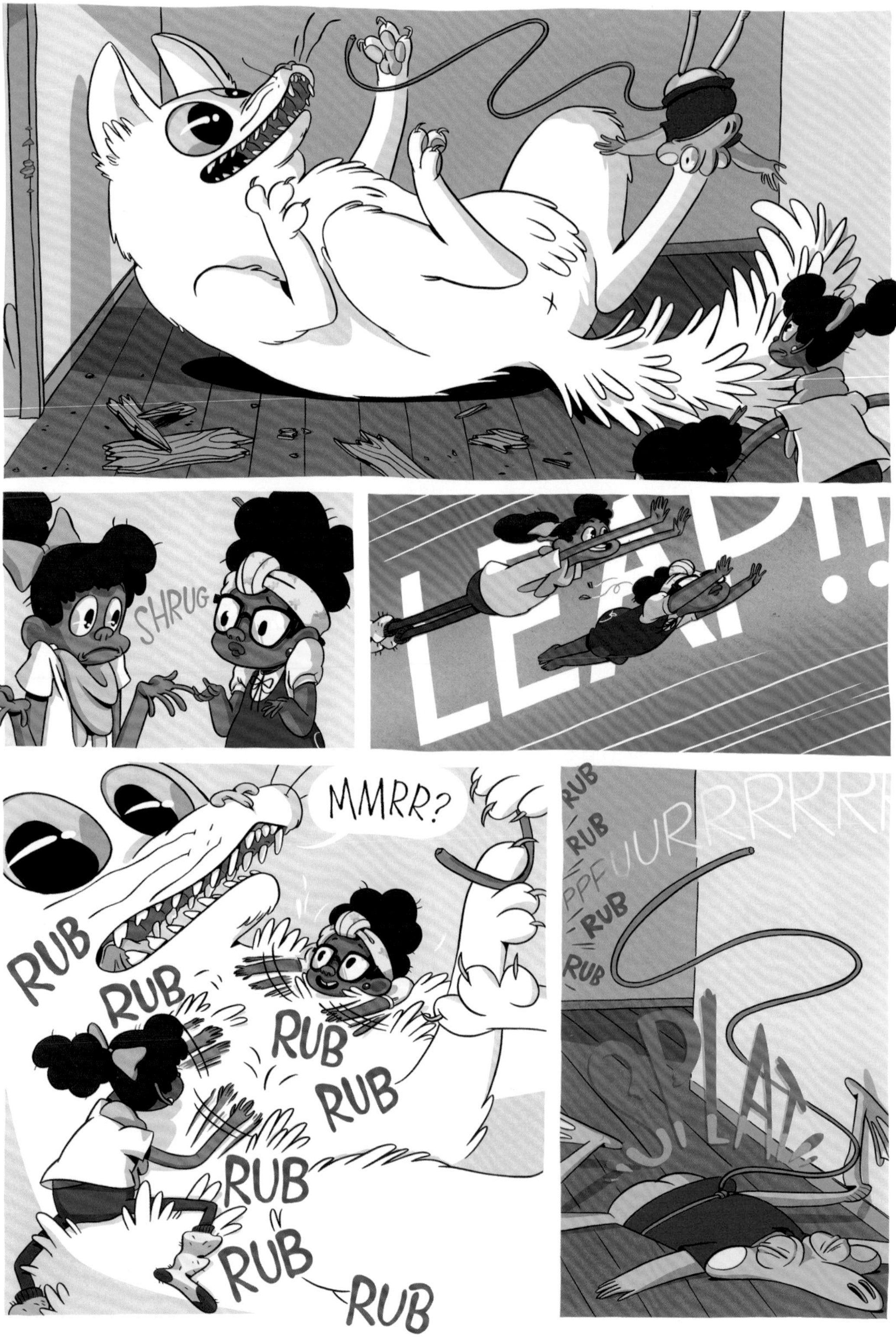
SHRUG
LEAP!!
MMRR?
RUB
RUB
RUB
RUB
RUB
RUB
RUB
RUB
RUB
PPFUURRRRRR
RUB
RUB
SPLAT

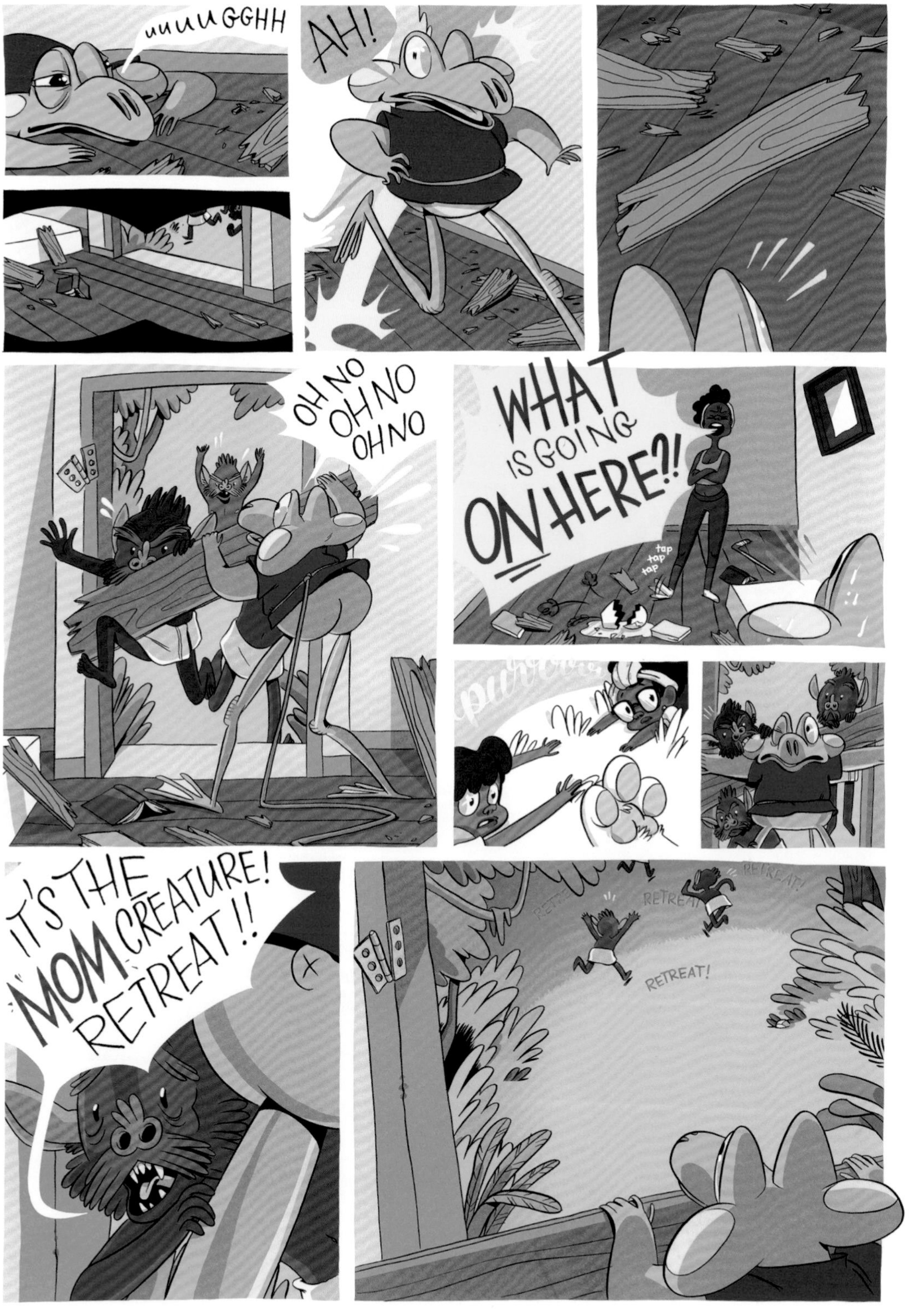
uuuuuGGHH
AH!
OH NO OH NO OH NO
WHAT IS GOING ON HERE?!
tap tap tap
IT'S THE MOM CREATURE! RETREAT!!
RETREAT!
RETREAT
RETREAT!

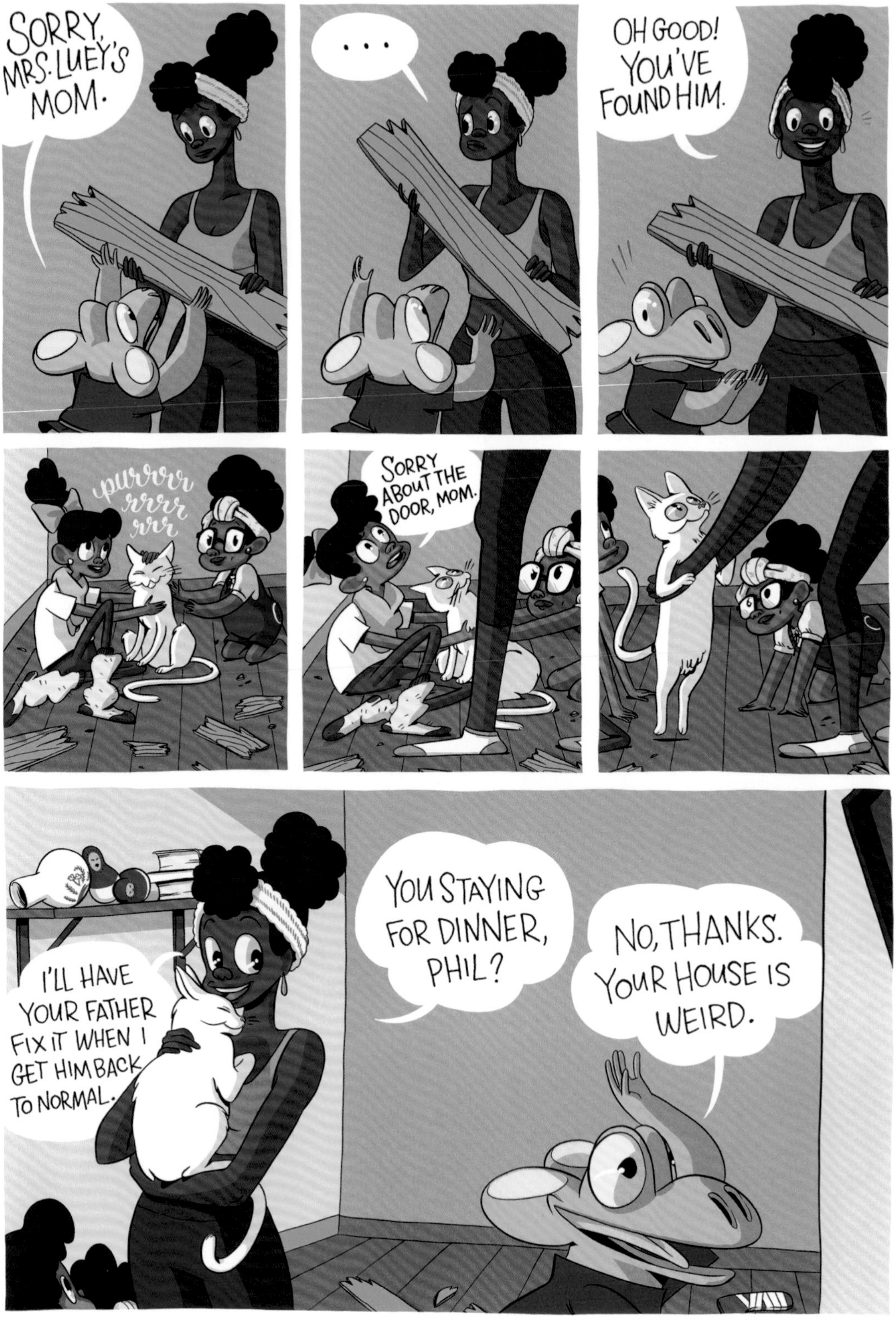
SORRY, MRS. LUEY'S MOM.
. . .
OH GOOD! YOU'VE FOUND HIM.
purrrrr rrrrr rrr
SORRY ABOUT THE DOOR, MOM.
I'LL HAVE YOUR FATHER FIX IT WHEN I GET HIM BACK TO NORMAL.
YOU STAYING FOR DINNER, PHIL?
NO, THANKS. YOUR HOUSE IS WEIRD.

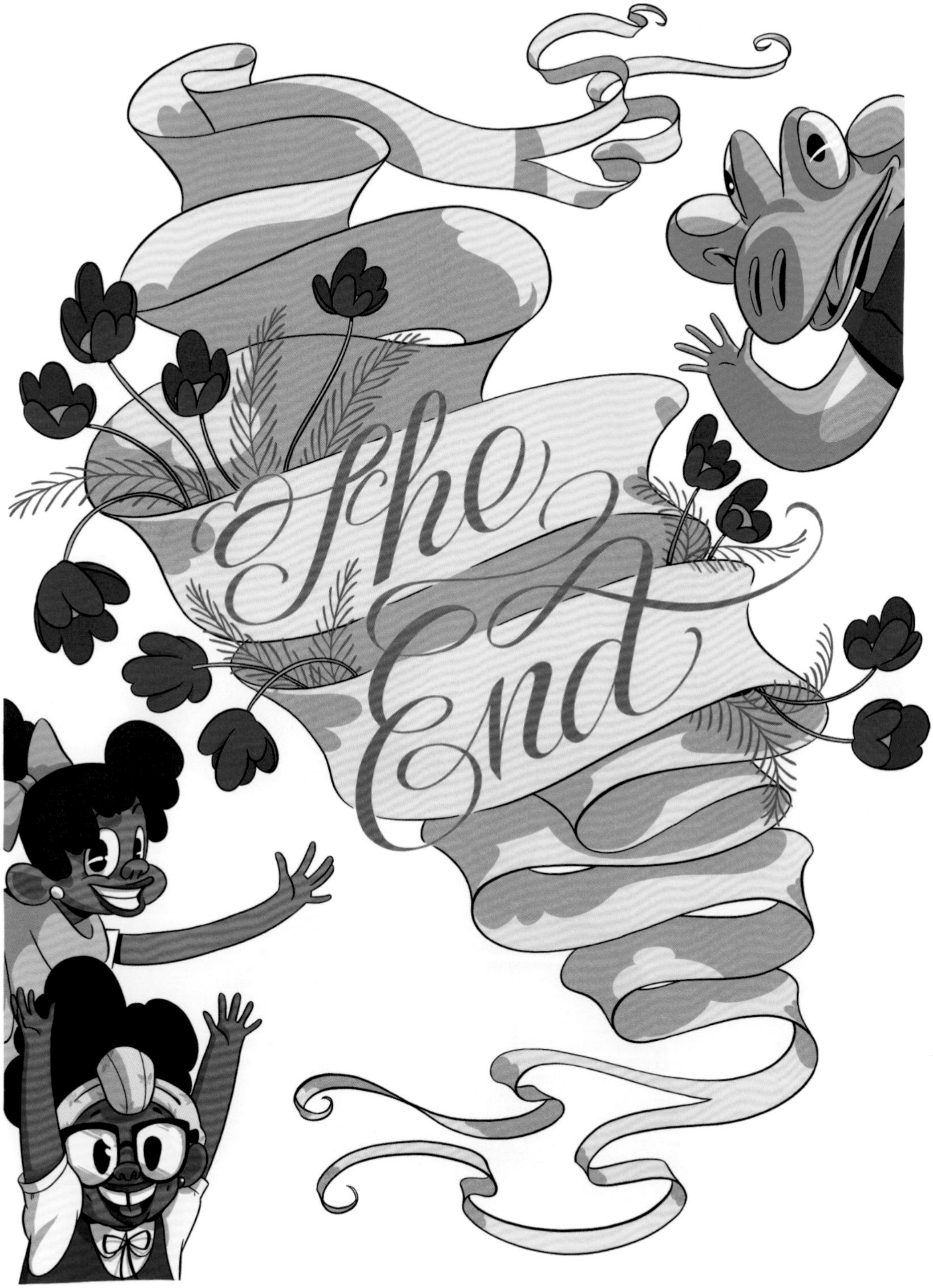
The End

ANATOMY OF A GOBLIN

"GOBLIN" IS A MISNOMER OF SORTS. THE CREATURES LIVING IN LUEY'S AND MIRI'S LINEN CLOSET ARE ACTUALLY A SENTIENT FORM OF FUNGUS (MUSHROOM), AND NOT A MYTHOLOGICAL CREATURE AT ALL. NOT MUCH IS KNOWN ABOUT THEM.

AN ARTIST'S REPRESENTATION OF HOW WE THINK GOBLINS LOOK INSIDE.

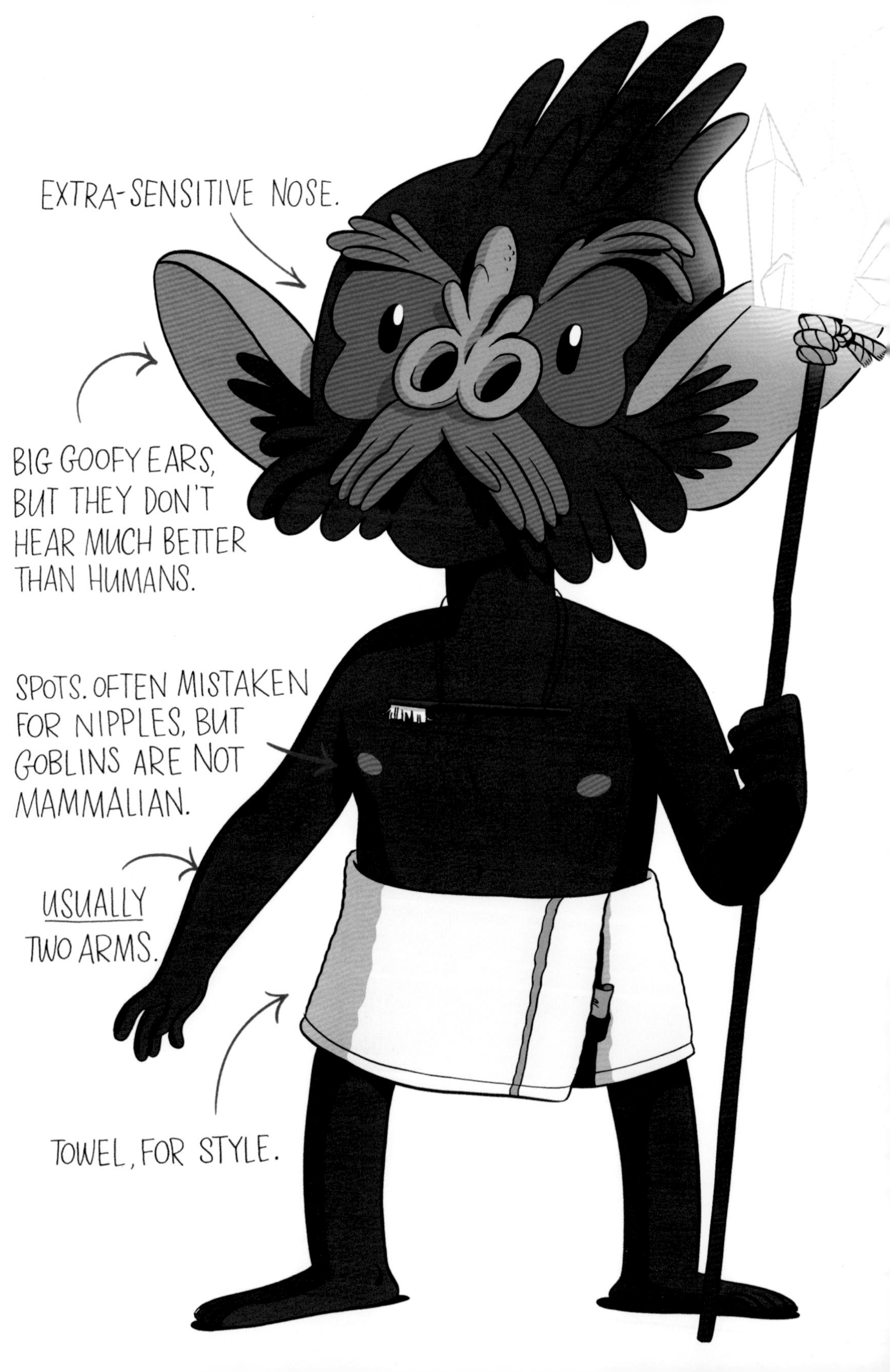
EXTRA-SENSITIVE NOSE.
BIG GOOFY EARS, BUT THEY DON'T HEAR MUCH BETTER THAN HUMANS.
SPOTS. OFTEN MISTAKEN FOR NIPPLES, BUT GOBLINS ARE NOT MAMMALIAN.
USUALLY TWO ARMS.
TOWEL, FOR STYLE.

THANKS TO ANNIE, ED AND HELEN, FOR ALL YOUR
HARD WORK. AND TO AVIV, FOR FEEDING ME,
CLOTHING ME AND MAKING SURE I SLEPT ONCE
IN A WHILE, DURING THE CREATION OF THIS
BOOK, (I LOVE YOU).

Oh yeah,
and for colouring
half the book for me!
xoxo

ABOUT THE AUTHOR

BRITT LIVES IN A CONCRETE CAVE IN TORONTO, ONTARIO WITH HER HUSBAND, THEIR TWO RESCUE CATS AND AN UNFORTUNATE COOKIE ADDICTION. HER GREATEST ACCOMPLISHMENT TO DATE IS HER "MERMAID HAIR". WHICH IS PREHENSILE AND MAKES A GREAT CUP OF COFFEE.